BARGAIN!

- A themed anthology -

Presented by
Creative Writing Institute

Dedication

by Jianna Higgins

This year's dedication is for all writers who have written a story and have not yet released it into the world. That short story or novel is your baby, lovingly pieced together, so when is the right time to let it leave home? The fear of criticism or rejection is universal, so how can you increase your confidence?

1. Don't compare yourself to published authors. If you compare yourself to Nora Roberts, you're likely to feel woefully inadequate. Be fair to yourself.
2. Release negative messages of the past, especially, "I'm not good enough." If you've tried something and failed, keep learning and move forward. It's not over until you quit.
3. Find another writer and help them. This gives you perspective on the value of what you have to offer.
4. Accept all feedback. Positives will make you feel good. Negatives will keep you grounded and make your work stronger.
5. Don't say, "I want to be a published author." Say, "I'm taking steps to becoming a published author."
6. Once you've finished your story, have it critiqued by another writer. Unless friends or family members are published authors, they

cannot offer an expert opinion.

7. Have your work professionally edited. Even experienced authors do not edit their own work.
8. Create a pseudonym if it makes you feel safer.
9. Self-publish or query an agent/publishing house with a high quality product.

If you write, then you're a writer. If your dream is to be a published author, you must publish. What do you have to lose? Walk in confidence to gain the life you want.

http://jiannahiggins.com/

CONTENTS

Acknowledgements

by Deborah Owen, CEO

This collection contains three short story winners, two honorable mentions, and ten finalists in the CWI annual short story contest. In addition, we have stories from the judges, CEO, previous winners and 5 best selling authors, making a total of 30 stories in various genres, but all using the same theme sentence. What an interesting anthology!

First and foremost, we would like to thank Southern Star Publications and its head editor, Jay Hirst, for support and publication.

Thank you, Jianna Higgins, for designing the cover, editing and proofreading, and thanks to Nicky Hirst, who kindly proofread the entire book.

Thank you Harvey Stanbrough for writing the Foreword.

Behind the scenes are the judges who gave their time willingly. Without them there would be no contest! Thank you, each and every one!

Short Story Contest Judges
Head judge: Jo Popek
Coordinating judge: Jianna Higgins
Judge: L. Edward Carroll
Judge: Emily-Jane Hills Orford

This year's theme is, *"I got more than I bargained for."* Creative Writing Institute proudly presents its 2015 Anthology – **BARGAIN!** Read and enjoy.

Foreword

I got more than I bargained for!
by Harvey Stanbrough

In my experience, traditionally a foreword is used to introduce what comes after it. However, in this case, I was engaged more to explain my own process. Apparently the folks at Creative Writing Institute see me as "the most serious writer" they've ever met, so, much of this foreword will be my take on how to get serious about writing and what it takes to become a good hobbyist writer or a professional fiction writer.

It certainly fits the theme of this anthology, because once I learned what I learned, I got a great deal more than I bargained for.

I began writing at the age of six. During my life, I have been a preacher, a working cowboy, a US Marine, a laborer both in the oilfields of southeast New Mexico and with a landscaping company in Indiana, a college instructor, a proofreader for a major publisher of computer books and educational materials, a freelance copyeditor, a writing instructor and a lecturer.

In my heyday as a speaker at writers' conferences, I hit eighteen in one year. During all that time, I told people I was a writer, but in actuality, I wasn't. I was one who wrote when he had a chance, and the chances didn't come around very often. But more importantly, when they did, I didn't take advantage of them.

I didn't actually become a professional writer until October 21, 2014. That's the day on which I wrote the first word of my first novel. At that point I had been writing at least one short story per week since April 16, 2014, so it wasn't like I didn't know my way around a keyboard.

I revisited an old acquaintance, USA Today's bestselling author, Dean Wesley Smith, and Dean told me about Heinlein's Rules. (To see an annotated copy of Heinlein's Rules, which by the way are not only for science fiction, please visit **http://www.HarveyStanbrough.com/Downloads**, and then click Heinlein's Rules. It's free.) I've been following Heinlein's Rules ever since. They are the simplest rules in the universe, and yet the most difficult to follow. As Robert Heinlein said, that's probably why there are so many aspiring writers and so few professionals.

At about the same time, Dean Smith also introduced me to a technique called *Writing Off Into the Dark*. (Visit **http://www.HarveyStanbrough.com/lecture-series** and scroll down to read about Course 12.) From then on, I haven't looked back.

But let's look at the numbers. Whatever else they do, numbers do not lie.

Before April 16, 2014, in around sixty years, I wrote a lot of traditional poetry, essays, articles and so on, but only about 10 short stories.

Since April 16, 2014, I have written around 80 short stories.

Before October 21, 2014, I had never written

a novel.

Since October 21, 2014, I have written nine novels and a novella.

Before April 16, 2014 — again, in around sixty years — I wrote approximately 200,000 words of published poetry, essays, articles and short fiction. So, something over 3300 words per year. That's like ten words a day. Devoted, eh?

From April 16, 2014 to April 15, 2015, I wrote 476,176 words of published fiction. That still averages only 1300 words per day. A little over an hour's work.

And from January 1, 2015, to present as I write this (September 17, 2015), I have written 491,883 words of published fiction, and there are still three months and thirteen days to go in this year.

Many people are amazed by the facts and figures. I don't get that.

I'm a writer. Why wouldn't I write? Why can't a writer also have a work ethic?

Funny story: I visited my doctor for a routine office call. As I was leaving, he smiled and said, "So, are you still writing?"

I just looked at him for a moment, then I smiled, too, and said, "Yep. And how about you. You're still practicing medicine, huh?"

We both got a laugh out of it, but it really isn't all that funny. Unfortunately, many people (yes, even writers) look at writing as an "elevated" profession. They also look at it as if it can never be more than an avocation, a hobby. They're wrong on both accounts. Incredibly, ridiculously wrong.

In almost every profession or job, you are required to spend eight hours per day, five days per week doing that job. Nobody questions that or thinks it strange. But if I spend only three hours writing, five days per week, and write only 50 weeks per year (I take two weeks for vacation), I will write 750,000 words in a year. That would equate to fifteen 50,000 word novels. It would equate to a hundred and twenty-five 6,000 word short stories or two hundred and fifty 3,000 word short stories.

And everyone would think I'm a blazing fast writer.

No. *shrug… I just spend three hours per day doing my job.

But what if you have to work a "real" job to make ends meet?

Been there, done that. If you want to also write, keep a journal for a week. Figure out, in fifteen-minute increments, how you spend your time. Be honest. It's just for you. You'll be surprised at how much spare time you actually have. Then, when you can carve out fifteen minutes, a half-hour, or an hour, sit down and write. It's as easy as that.

Say you are able to write "only" one hour per day. That's a thousand words (1,000 words per hour is only 17 words per minute). Even if you did that only five days per week for fifty weeks and took two weeks off, you still would have written 5,000 words per week and 250,000 words in a year. That's five 50,000 word novels, etc. You can do the math.

But what if you could write only a half-hour

per day, five days per week? Oh, goodness. Then you could write 125,000 words in a year.

Whatever you do, if you want to be a writer, then be a writer. Now a researcher is not a writer. An editor is not a writer. A person who's thinking about being a writer someday is not a writer. *A writer is a person who puts new words on the page.*

At Creative Writing Institute, there are good courses and a staff chock full of caring people who are waiting to help. Visit **http://www.CreativeWritingInstitute.com** and browse. You'll see what I mean.

If you visit my website you can sign up for my free Pro Writers blog on writing. Read my Daily Journal, in which I gripe and grouse my way through my own writing process, enjoy the writing tips, my Free Short Story of the Week, and my own daily, monthly and annual numbers.

Enjoy the anthology. In this, you most definitely will get more than you bargained for.

***

BIO: Harvey Stanbrough is an award-winning writer and poet. He's fond of saying he was born in New Mexico, seasoned in Texas, and baked in Arizona. After 21 years in the US Marine Corps, he managed to sneak up on a BA degree at Eastern New Mexico University in Portales in 1996. Because he is unable to do otherwise, he splits his writing personality with his persona, *Gervasio Arrancado*, who writes magic realism. Harvey's former personas include *Nicolas Z "Nick" Porter*, who wrote spare, descriptive, mainstream fiction, and *Eric Stringer,*

who wrote the fiction of an unapologetic neurotic. Harvey now writes in those formats himself.
http://harveystanbrough.com

Let Me Tell You a Story

by Michael Coolen
First Place Winner 2015 Contest

After Friday evening prayers, the people of the West African village of Ndiougue gather around an ancient jackfruit tree. The surrounding wooden benches are worn smooth by centuries of use. For as long as the village has existed, its inhabitants gather weekly to rest, chat, and listen to the village Jaliba play a 21-stringed kora and tell stories.

A young boy named Babukar waited near the bench where the Jaliba traditionally sat, hoping to be noticed, waiting for the day when he could become the Jaliba. Thousands of fruit bats nested in the mango trees beyond the security fences. Babu loved the sound of the bats whose chirruping was so loud that it drowned out the sounds of moaning lions beyond the trees. The music of a lute-like kora, announced the arrival of the Jaliba, who sat next to Babu and waited for the crowd to grow silent. A hush fell.

"Let me tell you a story," began the old Jaliba. "I don't know if this story is true or not, but the person who told it was an honorable man, and I have no reason to doubt him."

The Jaliba always begins the same way, Babu thought. *Let me tell you a story.*

"The man who told me this story was the

Jaliba before me, and he could recite our history for hundreds of rains, stretching back to the time of Koche Barma, the wisest man who ever lived.

"There was a time, a long time ago," he continued, "when there was much trouble in the land. The king's name was Daou Demba, and he was a brutal ruler. He banned gathering in groups and eating freshly slaughtered meat. He required new brides to spend three days in his bed before moving in with their husbands. The people hated him.

"Daou Demba was so afraid of challengers that he ordered all the men in the kingdom to shave their heads to show humility. Anyone who disobeyed would be whipped on his head until the hair was completely gone. All the men did as they were ordered, all but Koche Barma." The Jaliba began singing a praise song.

No man was his equal.
No man was equal to Koche Barma.
The big tree has fallen and all the birds have
scattered.

"Instead of shaving his head completely," the Jaliba said, "Koche Barma kept four raised tufts of hair. When the king, Daou Demba, heard of it, he was furious, and he ordered spies to find out what the tufts of hair represented. The spies returned a few days later, having learned nothing.

"Two days later the king received a message from a woman who said she would reveal Koche Barma's secrets. Daou Demba knew the woman. She was the widow of Koche Barma's older brother.

When the brother died, tradition dictated that Koche Barma take her as his second wife and support her and her child.

"Daou Demba ordered his men to bring her to the compound. She arrived two hours later, along with her adult son. Both dressed in expensive apparel, a sign that Koche Barma had honored the duty to his brother.

"I will give you ten pounds of gold if you tell me about Koche Barma's hair," the king said.

"Each tuft represents a moral truth," the woman replied. "The first says you should love your second wife, but do not trust her. The second says that one's adopted son is never one's own son. The third says that it is important to listen to the advice of elders, and the fourth tuft says that a ruler is neither a friend nor a protector."

Daou Demba was furious when he heard the last saying.

"Bring the traitor to me immediately," he shouted. When they had departed, one of the elders of the court, respected by the king for his wisdom and foresight, approached Daou Demba.

"If you kill him," the elder said, "many bad things could happen. First, the death of the wisest man in the kingdom would be an irreparable loss to the people. Second, executing him could foster resentment from the people who love and respect him." Other advisors agreed, and by the time the soldiers had dragged Koche Barma into the court, the king had changed his mind.

"We would have returned sooner," one of

the soldiers said, "but Koche Barma insisted in dressing in fine garments to visit your highness."

"No!" yelled the son of the woman who betrayed him.

Koche Barma smiled as the step-son rushed before the king.

"He is wearing my garments! Please undress him before you slay him so that no blood stains my raiment."

The king descended the throne steps and confronted Koche Barma. "I know the secret of your hair tufts," he said. "Do you deny one tuft stands for a ruler that can be neither friend nor protector?"

Koche Barma responded calmly. "Despite the services I have rendered you and the kingdom for decades, you have condemned me to death simply because I won't reveal secrets that I have the right to keep to myself. Don't your actions prove I am correct that a ruler can be neither a friend nor a protector? And is it not true," he continued, "that the woman who betrayed my secrets to you was my second wife, whom I try to love, but do not trust?"

"Amin (so be it)," nearby advisors whispered, seated in the shadows.

"And is it not true," Koche Barma said, "that one of my tufts states an adopted son is never one's own? And did not my adopted son just kneel before you and beg you to strip me naked before killing me so that no blood would stain his garments?"

The king cast a disgusted look at the wife who wasn't a wife and the son who wasn't a son. In the corner of the room, the elder advisor caught Daou Demba's eyes and nodded affirmation ever so slightly, but Koche Barma witnessed the subtle exchange.

"And I suspect it's also true that the wise advice of an elder diffused your passion before you had me killed for an unjust cause," Koche Barma said.

"Amin," was whispered in the crowd.

The king, Daou Demba, stood quietly for a few moments, pondering the situation that had turned on him. *I got more than I bargained for*, he said to himself. He walked back to his throne, turned around and addressed the court.

"Confiscate the possessions of this vile woman and her equally vile son," he said. "Give them some water and a little food, and banish them into the Wulo Kono, where the wild dogs live."

Daou Demba released Koche Barma, who returned home to offer wisdom and advice to all who sought it. Years passed, and Koche Barma eventually forced the king out of office and banished him to the Wulo Kono… but that's another story," the old Jaliba said.

Again, the Jaliba sang a short fragment from the praise song.

There was no man equal to him.
There was no man equal to him.
There was no man equal to Koche Barma.
But the big tree has fallen and all the birds have scattered now.

As he finished the last note, all the villagers

shouted "Amin" and "So be it" to reaffirm the moral truth of the story. They chatted about it all evening while gathering their belongings and returning to their huts, but Babu remained seated, unwilling to end the magic spell just yet. When he looked up, he noticed the Jaliba standing next to him with his 21-stringed kora.

"Did you like the story, Babu?" Jaliba said.

"Yes. It was a wonderful story."

"Your parents have spoken to me. They have asked me to accept you as an apprentice. Would you like that, Babu?"

"Yes, Jaliba. I would like that very much."

At that very moment, the sound of a distant roaring lion caught their attention.

"There," whispered the Jaliba. "Hear that? You probably think that was a lion, but it was not. It was the spirit of Sundiata, which means, 'the hungry lion.' Sundiata says you will be a great Jaliba."

Babu's glittering eyes peered at the old man. "Who is Sundiata?"

The old Jaliba smiled at the boy, sat down and strummed his kora. "Let me tell you a story."

***

The Silver's Secret

by Julie Fox
Second Place Winner 2015 Contest

The shopkeeper, a sprightly old man with a shock of white hair, returned from the back room holding a small wooden box. Inside, a dull silver ring sat nestled on a green velvet cushion. He placed it on the counter in front of Leah, hugging the box with his hands.

"This is a very special ring," he said, smiling down on it. "It will be perfect to write about for your history project. The others I showed were replicas of jewelry worn by kings and queens, but this one is different. It …"

"It'll do for me," Leah said, snatching the ring from its cushion and dashing out the door. She barreled into the clammy night, passed under the sign that read Unique Gifts and Antiques, and sprinted down the empty street. She could hear the shopkeeper shouting.

"Stop! You don't know what you're …"

Leah kept running, easily distancing herself from the man's shouts until all she could hear was the wind in her ears. As she ran, she pressed the small band between her fingers until her hand went numb. *Yeah, this'll do just fine,* she thought, and flew on the wings of adrenaline to her front porch.

As she waited for her breaths to slow under

the glow of the porch light, she squinted at the ring in her hand. It was just a thin silver band, like the wedding band her parents wore, but the inside bore a graceful inscription in a language she didn't understand. She dug her house key from her pocket and unlocked the door, nudging it open slowly. The living room was dark and silent, and she tiptoed up the stairs to her room and locked the door.

Leah sat amidst the pile of sheets and stuffed animals on her bed and slid the warm ring on her finger. A perfect fit. She held her hand out to admire it. "So, 'Ethan never gets you anything,' huh?" she said in a whiny imitative voice, and then smiled. "Look at what he just got me."

The next day, Leah walked into school with a confident smile. When she reached her friends in the hallway, she brushed her long brown hair back with her ringed hand.

Her friends stopped talking and looked at Leah with wide eyes. "Is that from Ethan?" Nicole asked, grabbing Leah's hand.

Jessica rubbed it, squinting. "It's dull and scratched up," she said, furrowing her brows. "Why would he give you a trashy old ring?"

Leah took her hand back. "It was his great-grandmother's," she said. "I think it has character."

"Hey, at least he gave her something," Nicole said, slamming her locker shut. "The last time Devin gave me anything was when he didn't want his old CD player anymore."

"Look at what's written inside," Leah said, trying to pull the ring off, but it didn't move. It grew warm under her grasp. "Huh… I guess it's stuck." She tugged at it again, puzzled. It had been the perfect size the night before.

Jessica smiled at Leah, displaying perfectly straight teeth. "Hey, at least now we know you didn't make him up."

Leah smiled back, but fear and dislike fluttered in her chest. She wondered why she even wanted to impress Jessica with a fake boyfriend. And why couldn't she remove the ring? After school, she walked into her house to hear clanging sounds in the kitchen.

"How was school?" her mom called.

"Fine," Leah said. She had twisted the ring round her finger all day and each time she tugged, it grew warm, as though enchanted. A pit of dread was growing in her stomach.

"Can you go to the store for some butter? I'm making cookies for a lady at work, and your father used the last stick for the potatoes last night."

Leah leaned against the door frame. "Are you sure we don't have any? I have homework."

Her mother checked again. "I'm sure. I just looked through the entire, oh …" She looked up at her daughter and back to the box of butter sitting in the middle of the top shelf. "I swear, that wasn't there two minutes ago." She reached in and took out the box, looking at it closely. "Wow, I don't even remember buying this brand. I think I'm going crazy."

The ring pricked Leah's finger in a sudden burst of heat when her mother found the butter.

She rubbed it. "No problem," she said as she turned to go upstairs.

"I hope these cookies turn out better than the last few batches," her mother was saying behind her.

Upstairs, Leah sat at her desk and tried to bury thoughts of the ring under math homework. She scratched through her equations, barely able to concentrate, her eyes resting more on her hand than on her small-lettered work.

Why won't it come off? Why won't it come off? played constantly in her head. She threw her pencil down, went into the bathroom and dabbed liquid citrus soap around the ring. She pulled and twisted the ring under cold water, and yanked harder when nothing happened. When her finger began to burn and turn grey, she stopped, the pain receded, and normal flesh color returned.

Leah went to school the next day with unbrushed hair and a rumpled jacket she'd slept in. She'd spent the night curled on her bed, fighting off panic attacks. The pretty ring she had stolen to maintain the boyfriend lie now reminded her of every haunted heirloom story she had ever read. After resolving to return to the old man's shop despite the trouble she'd be in, she had dozed off clutching one of her teddy bears.

Her friends exchanged glances at her sudden transformation. "What happened?" Jessica asked at lunch. "Did Prince Charming dump you?"

Leah scowled and twisted the ring. "No."

Nicole looked at her with concern. "Well,

what's wrong? You're so quiet today. And you keep twirling your ring."

Leah took her hand away from her ring and tried to soften her expression. "I'm fine. I'm just... worried about the math test."

Nicole groaned theatrically. "I know. I wish Mr. Davis would cancel the test."

"I wish he'd have a car wreck," Jessica said. "I hate him and his impossible tests."

"Yeah," Leah said absentmindedly, thinking of the old man at the antique shop. Why would he have a ring like that? Maybe he didn't know about it. If so, she was really in trouble. She sank lower in her chair.

"Wow, you guys are cruel," Nicole said, raising an eyebrow. "At least I studied."

After lunch, students chatted in math class and reread notes as they waited. Mr. Davis was late, and Leah sat hunched over her desk, wincing, as the ring burned like fire.

An English teacher entered. "Class, Mr. Davis has been in a car accident," she said, her voice quick as if she had just heard the news herself. "He's okay, but they're taking him to the hospital for a checkup."

The stone of anxiety in Leah's stomach grew into a boulder.

The teacher walked over to Mr. Davis' spotless desk and plopped down. "I heard there was supposed to be a test today, so use this period as a study hall. No talking, please." The teacher ran fingers through her hair and pulled out her iPhone.

Jessica poked Leah. "Hey, he's okay," she whispered, although her eyes were wide.

Leah stared back, her face white. "I think I'm going to be sick," she said, and ran from the room. That afternoon, Leah ran back to the antique shop. She really did feel sick, and only the desperate hope that the shopkeeper could help kept her from collapsing and vomiting. A slow rain began to fall as Leah arrived at the store and pushed open the door. Panting, she wrapped her arms around herself. "Hello?" she called in the empty room. Chipped furniture, outdated yard decorations, and shelves of antique junk crowded around her.

"Back here," the shopkeeper called from the back room. "I'll be right with you." He came out a moment later, and adjusted his spectacles when he saw Leah's slumping form. "Ah," he said in patronizing humor, "I thought you'd come back."

Leah glared at him. "This ring I took ..." She held up her hand.

"You mean the ring you stole."

"It's magic. It's cursed. It won't come off. It ..." Leah's voice faltered and tears jumped into her eyes.

The old man leaned on his counter and looked at her with amusement. "I tried to tell you it was special when you ran off with it."

Tears streaked down Leah's cheeks. "Special? I can't get it off! You can have it back, just help me get it off! Please. It burns and turns my finger grey."

The shopkeeper straightened and folded his arms. "Hold on. Let me tell you what I was trying to say last night."

Leah sniffled and fell silent.

"The ring isn't cursed. It's enchanted. It gives you the power to grant peoples' wishes." He threw out an arm. "You're like a genie!"

"But I don't want …"

"With that ring on, you'll be immortal, un-ageing, and, except when you actually try to take it off, impervious to injury." He waggled his eyebrows at her. "Pretty good deal, eh?"

Leah stamped her foot. "I don't want any of that! I just want to get this stupid ring off and get back to my life!"

He held a hand out as if to calm her. "Okay, Missy. Whatever you want. Besides, the longer you keep that thing on, the more you'll belong to the spirit world. Eventually you won't even have a human body and you'll be forced to wander the earth in search of a master."

Leah's eyes widened in shock. "What?" she squeaked.

The old man laughed. "Oh, don't look like that. There's always a loophole. It has to do with that inscription on the inside."

"Tell me! What does it say?"

He cocked his head as if trying to solve a difficult problem. After a minute he shook his head. He shrugged. "Sorry. I can't tell you that."

Leah rushed toward the counter, holding her hands out in supplication. "Please," she sobbed, "tell me what to do. I can't be a spirit. I have to get it off! Anything. I'll give you anything you want.

Please!"

He smiled mischievously. "Well, if you work here to pay off your debt, I might be persuaded to talk. Or I might not."

Leah wiped her nose and took a shaky breath as relief spread through her body. Stealing the ring to fake the boyfriend story seemed stupid and petty now. As she looked at the ring through teary eyes, her mother's favorite phrase bubbled into her mind. She almost laughed at how well it fit her situation.

I got more than I bargained for, she thought.

***

Helping Granny Lomax

by Randa Sansing
Third Place Winner 2015 Contest

Summer vacation had just started, and Ronny and I were looking for ways to earn money for new bicycles. I had outgrown mine, and Ronny's was worn out, held together with duct tape and wire. Money was tight in 1964 in rural Alabama. A kid without a bike was a kid who couldn't get around. There weren't that many jobs available for two boys, ages eleven and twelve so we spread the word in the neighborhood.

Finally, things started looking up. Granny Lomax sent a message that she had some yard work for us to do. Ronnie lived with his grandparents about a half mile away. He rode his bicycle to my house, and we rode together another mile to Granny's house.

When we arrived at 10 a.m., Granny was waiting on the front porch. She wasn't really related to either of us, but everybody around there called her Granny. She was an elderly widow and had her own way of doing things. "Good morning, Charles Nicholas Brown and Ronald Avery Johnson."

"Most people call me Nick," I said.

"I go by Ronny."

"Humph. I'm surprised your parents would give you such dignified names and then allow them to be chopped up and most of it tossed out."

I didn't say a word, but Ronny came right back.

"My parents tossed me out with the name, so I don't guess they cared much."

"Maybe they had their reasons for leaving. Anyway, they left you with good grandparents so you're still mighty lucky."

Ronny nodded in agreement.

I didn't think it was her business what names we used, but I was taught not to talk back to adults. I was pretty sure that went double for adults who were as old and wrinkled as Granny.

"Your first job is to rake these leaves in the front yard." She handed each of us a rake and pointed to an old wheelbarrow. "When you get it good and full, push it around to the back of the house and dump it in the gulley."

It seemed pretty easy at first—rake up a pile, fill the wheel barrow, and take turns dumping it, but after twenty-five loads, my back started hurting and my arms were getting numb. It was becoming obvious… I got more than I bargained for.

Ronny looked at me, sweat running down his face. "Hey, Nick, reckon we could take a break?"

"We can't stop before she does. Look at her. She's been pulling weeds like a maniac ever since we started. Surely, she can't last much longer."

Finally, right before my arms went into total paralysis, we emptied the last wheel barrow and the front yard was done!

"Okay, boys, you can stop for a little while,"

Granny said as she brought us a glass of ice water. We rocked in the rocking chairs on her front porch and sipped cold water while she went back into the house. She wasn't even breathing hard.

A few minutes later, she came back with a plate of peanut butter and jelly sandwiches and two Cokes. After we washed our hands at the outside faucet, we rocked and ate lunch. I guess Granny ate hers in the house.

By the time we finished, she was loading stuff into a wobbly old grocery cart. We watched as she loaded a five gallon bucket full of scuffed up golf balls, a golf club, and an empty five gallon bucket. Lastly, she put in a paper bag, rolled down at the top.

"Let's go down to the pasture, boys. I need you to chase some balls for me. Hitting golf balls is good exercise for my arms."

We looked at each other, thinking she must be kidding. She wasn't. We scrambled after her as she headed toward the pasture, pushing the cart. This was one odd job that caught us completely by surprise. Living way out in the country on small farms, we'd never heard of anybody around there playing golf. Heck, we'd barely heard of golf.

Ronny took the cart from Granny. Leading us through a wooden gate, she headed to a flat section of well-grazed pasture. As we stopped under a huge water oak tree, I heard the familiar gurgling sound of the creek close by. Every pasture in the valley had a slice of that creek running through it.

Granny picked her spot and then took out

the bucket full of balls and poured them on the ground. She handed each of us an empty bucket and told us the direction she planned to hit the balls. "Spread out!" she yelled.

I rolled my eyes at Ronny as we walked. "No point in going too far," he said. "How far can she hit 'em? She's an old lady." We found out real quick.

He went left and I went right, both of us stopping about twenty yards out. She hit the first ball in his direction, and it zipped over his head traveling at the speed of light. He took off after it, and I backed up another twenty yards. The next one came toward me, and I barely had a split second to dodge it.

I heard Ronny yell, "Yeehaw!"

Granny cackled.

For the next hour, we dodged and chased golf balls while Granny laughed and hollered at us. Sometimes it was a line drive going fifty miles an hour. Others flew over our heads or zipped past us at warp speed. Ronny, being a competitor and a good athlete, thought he could stop the balls. He kept dropping to the ground, trying to roll on top of them. I was just trying to avoid death or serious injury.

Looking at Granny through sweaty eyeballs, she appeared to be riding on a broom, wearing a pointed hat, and swooping down to whack another ball at us.

When she finally ran out of ammunition, she yelled, "Go find 'em. I can't afford to buy new ones."

So we took off in every direction looking for the balls under bushes, in the creek, plopped in cow patties. Pee-yew! What a way to earn a buck! We found most of them and dropped into the buckets.

"Come up here under the tree and cool off now," Granny called.

Wet with sweat, we flopped down, slumping against that big tree trunk, and it felt like a million dollars. Taking off my shoes and socks, I looked around for the cows, but didn't see any. Of course not! When they saw her coming with that grocery cart, they hightailed it out of there. Too bad we hadn't been that smart.

"How long you been hitting golf balls?" Ronny asked.

"Oh, my son, Wayne, left them here a few years back when he moved up north. I get out and hit them every once in a while. It's a lot more fun when I don't have to run 'em down myself. I don't know when I've laughed so hard. You two are a hoot to watch."

I couldn't think of anything nice to say about the experience, so I decided to keep my trap shut. Just leaned and rested, wondering which part of my body was gonna hurt the worst tomorrow.

At least Ronny was a good sport and pretended he had enjoyed the game of deadly dodge ball.

Granny took the paper bag from the cart and pulled out a loaf-bread sack full of homemade tea cakes. They were a pale yellow, with slightly browned crispy edges. While she poured grape

Kool-Aid into three Tupperware glasses, she told us to help ourselves to the cookies.

After we had stuffed ourselves, Granny said, "Why don't you boys get in that creek and splash around? It'll be good for your muscles."

"We don't have any more clothes," I said.

"You think those will disappear if they get wet?"

"Okay, why not?" Ronny said, and he was already heading toward the water. We took off our shirts and hung them on a bush before jumping in. The fact that it was only knee deep didn't matter. Icy cold, right down from the mountain, it changed sweat to chill bumps in an instant. Once my skin adjusted to the cold and my teeth stopped chattering, it felt terrific. After a few minutes of kicking and splashing, the tired went right out of my muscles. We lay in the water until we were completely relaxed.

When we saw Granny loading up the grocery cart, we put our shirts on and headed back to the oak tree. After we got our shoes on, we started for the house, with me pushing the cart this time.

Granny said that was enough for today and gave each of us two dollars.

"Thank you. Let us know if you need us to do any more chores," I said.

She said she would and waved to us as we rode off on our bikes.

I asked Ronny, "How old do you think she really is?"

"She's s'posed to be in her eighties," he said,

"but I'm beginning to think an alien took possession of her body and the alien is lean and mean and maybe in his twenties."

We both laughed.

"How much longer do you think she'll live?" I said.

"I don't know, but I bet she won't stop one minute ahead of time."

"I've never seen anybody like Granny. I thought she was trying to hit us with those golf balls. Reckon why she acts different from other grownups?"

After he thought about it, Ronnie said, "I bet'cha it's being free that makes her different. When you're a kid, you're not free; somebody's always telling you what to do. When you grow up, you're not free because you have to work and all that, but if you can make it to be as old as Granny Lomax, you can do whatever you darn well please. Nobody bothers you. I guess they figure you've earned it."

I could tell he admired her spunk. I should try to be more like Ronny. Always looking for the good in people. But right then, when I thought of Granny Lomax, all I could see was a cackling witch that tried to kill us. The day wasn't all bad though. The cookies were good, and we ended up with two dollars in our pockets. "Well, Nick, we're a little closer to new bicycles. Wonder if she'll ask us to work for her again."

"I wouldn't be surprised. There's a lot of stuff that needs doing around there, and she'll always have those dang golf balls."

**

Broken Glass

by Anne Skaltza
Honorable Mention 2015 Contest

Carole Santino sat in the office chair of her shop, Carole's Crafts, twisting a tissue in her hands. "I came in and saw the window in the back room had been broken by that brick." She pointed a red lacquered fingernail at the offending object. "Should've put in a security system like my ex-boyfriend said."

Officer Jeb Flitton nodded, clicked his pen and carefully wrote in his notebook. After five minutes of constant writing, he peered at the ceiling and watched a fat drop of water fall onto a large dark area of the carpet. He returned his gaze to the store owner and shook his head. "You should get that ceiling repaired soon or you'll have a real mess in here," he said. He tapped the pen on the open notebook. "Anything taken?"

"No. I looked around while I waited for you. Nothing was taken." She pointed toward a thick inside door. "And that door is still locked." She held up a small key. "See? You need this to lock or unlock both sides. When I'm here, I keep it unlocked. That door goes to the front room where I teach my classes and sell craft supplies. I empty the cash register every night." She pushed short brown curls off her face. "You know, I saved money to move here and open my business because it's a small, nice town, but it seems that I got more than I bargained for."

Flitton nodded in sympathy. He rummaged in his shirt pocket, and then snapped his fingers. "Forgot my cigarettes. Chief doesn't like me smoking on the job. Something about protocol or whatever. Guess you don't smoke, what with all the paints and stuff here, right?"

"Of course not."

"Right. Let me ask you something. Let's see. Where is it?" He shuffled through his notes, moving his mouth in silence.

Carole straightened her denim skirt and tapped her foot impatiently.

"Okay. Here it is. Your ex-boyfriend. Was he mad at you for something?"

She stopped mid-tap and frowned. "My ex? No way. The break-up was amicable. He took a job out of state and neither of us wanted a long distance relationship."

"Yeah, that can happen. I hear ya." He slowly turned and peered around the tiny back room that had one window and a heavy metal outside door. His eyes rested on a handwritten sign that rested on her desk. In large black letters, it stated a price increase for the children's classes. "You print that sign yourself?" he said. "That sure is nice work. My printing is like chicken scratches."

"Yes, yes, yes! Just please find out who did this." Carole sighed. "Look, if it'll move this along any faster, I'll explain. I made that sign after the last customer left. Then I got my coat and pocketbook and locked the door between the two rooms. Whoever broke the window wouldn't have been able to get into the front room." She waved her hand. "And as you can see, there's nothing to steal in here."

After several minutes, Officer Flitton finished note-taking, put his hat on and pulled his gloves from his jacket pocket. "Damp and cold, it is. Well, I'm going back to the station to type this up. Let me know if you think of anyone who might've done this."

She raised an eyebrow. "I really don't know anyone that well." She looked at the brick on the floor. "Aren't you going to take that? As evidence?"

"Oh, yeah. I guess I should," Flitton said.

He pulled a plastic bag from his pocket, put the brick inside, and zipped it shut. He pulled another plastic bag out and carefully placed a bloody shard of glass in it.

"Thank you, Officer. I have several things to do before I leave. I'm too rattled to have classes today. I'll have to get that window fixed, too."

"Yes, Ma'am. Good day."

She locked the door behind him, keeping the *Closed* sign turned out.

A few hours later, as Officer Jeb Flitton slowly made his way to the Hungry Haven Coffee Shoppe for his usual lunch of a BLT, side of fries, and decaf coffee, he passed a group of four women who chatted under their umbrellas. He stopped and tipped his hat. "And how is everyone today?" he asked. He knew they referred to him as "Dead Head Jeb," but he didn't mind.

Lisa Davenport spoke up. "Oh, we're all fine, Officer. Just talking about our children. You know how they are, out and about until we bother them on their cell phones. We're lucky Ms. Santino opened that shop and has those classes for them."

Flitton's dark eyebrows scrunched together. "Ms. Santino?"

Lisa laughed. "You know, the owner of Carole's Crafts."

The officer laughed and slapped his forehead, knocking his hat backward. He took his time straightening it before he answered. "Yes, of course. I was just there this morning. Somebody broke a window at her store."

The ladies gave a collective gasp. "Is she alright?"

"Oh yes. She's fine. It seems to have happened after she went home last evening. She found out this morning. No children's classes today."

Dani Brock crossed her arms and said, "I'm debating about sending Nicholas back since prices are going up."

Trish Malone said, "Humph. The classes are already expensive enough."

Flitton shrugged, tipped his hat again and headed into the coffee shop. His stomach was grumbling and he couldn't think on an empty stomach.

An hour later, feeling slower than usual,

Officer Flitton continued on to Doctor Sheila Evans' office a few doors down. After speaking with her a few minutes, he strode over to Carole's Crafts and knocked, thinking about the abundance of rainfall. Even his heavy jacket, hat, and gloves couldn't stop the dampness from penetrating. When Carole opened the door, he removed his hat and stepped inside. "Might I sit a bit?" he asked.

"Of course."

He pulled a chair out from the long craft table. "I think I know who threw the brick."

Carole's eyebrows shot up. "Already? I thought it would take days... or even months," she mumbled.

Flitton heard it, but let the remark pass. He stretched his legs and cleared his throat. For good measure, he cleared it again. "It dawned on me that the sign about the price increase was on your desk in the back room all night, right?"

"Yes."

"Well, here's the deal. Since you made the sign after everyone left, whoever saw that sign must have been the one who broke the window, right? I went into the coffee shop for lunch and there were four women talking near the entrance. Lisa, Dani, Trish, and... oh, someone else. Anyway, one of your students' parents mentioned the price increase, but I guess she could have heard about it from someone else. I realized that whoever threw the brick seemed to have cut their hand. How that happened is a mystery, though. But you see, there was blood on the shard of glass I took, so I visited the doctor here, Doctor Evans. Do you know her?"

"No."

"No? Well, she confirmed my suspicion that Dani Brocks' son, Nicholas, needed minor medical attention last night for a laceration -- her word, not mine -- on his right hand." Officer Flitton grinned and opened his arms wide. "So there you go!"

Carole's eyes widened. "So you already have the vandal? That was quite fast."

He brought his arms down and leaned forward. "Well, I thought I did, but ..."

"But what?"

"Just a minute," he said, feeling in his pockets. "Mind if I smoke?"

Carole dropped into a plastic chair and waved her hand. "Whatever."

"Oh, gee. I forgot my lighter."

"Here," she said as she tossed a book of matches to him.

He slowly opened a small plastic bag that held the remnants of a match and placed it on the single torn one in the book. "This morning, you said you don't smoke. Can't have matches around this place 'cause of the flammables. Remember?"

Carole reached over to grab the single match. "Give me that."

"No. I don't think so." Flitton pulled it out of her reach, dropped it back into the bag and got up. With two long strides, he opened the door and waved in a preteen boy and his mother, Dani Brock. Flitton walked over to Carole and firmly placed a beefy hand on her shoulder.

"This, as you may know, is Mrs. Dani Brock, and her son, Nicholas. Nicholas, tell Ms. Carole what you told me just before we came here."

Nicholas shuffled his feet and raised his head. "I was out late last night. Wasn't supposed to be though. Rode my bike behind the stores here, you know, lookin' for stuff. Dropped coins. You know. Stuff like that. I saw a guy in the back, locking the door. He saw me and ran. Then I looked in the window and saw smoke coming from something on the floor. Didn't have my cell phone with me so I thought quick. I grabbed a brick and threw it at the window. I tried to get inside to put out whatever was smoldering but I cut my hand on the glass trying to push the pieces in. Well, whatever was on the floor fizzled out, and that's when I saw the poster about the class prices going up. And, well, I hate doing arts and craft stuff."

Officer Flitton said, "Well, you obviously told your mother the classes were going to be more expensive. Why didn't you tell her what really happened?"

Nicholas' eyes darted over to his mother. "I wasn't supposed to be back there and I knew she'd be mad."

"Well," Flitton drawled, pressing his hand harder on Carole's shoulder, "I did a little researching of my own after I left this morning. I looked through the trash bin out back and saw a spent flare. Seems it fizzled because of your leaky ceiling in the back room. Thought I smelled some smoke earlier."

Carole knocked his hand off her shoulder and stood up. "It proves nothing! That little pipsqueak could have put it there," she said, pointing at Nicholas.

"By the way. I found your *ex-boyfriend*. Or should we say *accomplice in crime?* I got my kit and dusted the flare for fingerprints. There were two sets. One set I'm assuming will prove to be yours. The other set matches your ex-boyfriend's. It seems he's been in the legal systems for several years and lives close by. The last crime was for insurance fraud. My partner is questioning him at the station right now. A little more research showed you're six months behind on rent and utilities, so I guess you really did get more than you bargained for."

With startling swiftness, Officer Flitton slipped handcuffs on Carole while reading her rights. He turned to Mrs. Brock and said, "I guess you won't have to worry about paying higher prices now." And to Nicholas, he winked and said, "You lucked out, kid."

***

A Lucky Day

by Irene Wittig
Honorable Mention 2015 Contest

Bertie Grundle named her boy *Lawrence* in
hopes that he would turn out like Peter O'Toole in
Lawrence of Arabia, but her Lawrence had no sense
of adventure. He was more likely to be haunted by
the letter D since he was Divorced, Disappointed,
Depressed, Dull, and nearly Dead.

When he finally moved to a place of his own,
it was only so he wouldn't have to take a bus to
work. Even so, he returned home every Sunday
morning for a full English breakfast of oatmeal,
eggs, sausage, beans, tomato, buttered toast and
marmalade… a culinary custom Bertie imported
from her brief but thrilling trip to England to see
Peter O'Toole.

After breakfast, Bertie tried to interest him in
the news of the week, which usually failed. He
continued to come even after he married Dorothy,
as change was not something he accepted easily.
Dorothy was quite the opposite, flitting from one
idea to another until she left for good -- in
Lawrence's car while he was at work. Bertie tried to
convince him that change could work in his favor.
Hadn't he been thinking of getting a new car
anyway?

One Sunday morning, Bertie put her trash

cans in Lawrence's usual parking place just to shake him up a bit.

"I had to park in Kobloschenko's spot," Lawrence grumbled. "His shades are drawn so I assume he's away."

"Well, I wish he'd stay away," she said. "I'm sure he's a hit man for the Russian mob."

"Ma, really... what gave you that idea?"

Bertie scowled. "It's obvious. He doesn't keep regular hours, and unsavory characters come around at all hours of the day and night."

"His wife seems... nice."

"Oh, come on. Her name is Lulu. She has bleached hair and wears a mink coat," Bertie said, as if the details were proof of her culpability. "And she drives her son to school so some hit man doesn't come gunning for him." Bertie cut her fried egg and watched the yolk seep under the fried tomato. "The Russian mob is a lot more brutal than the Mafia, you know."

"You've been watching too much TV, Ma."

Bertie tucked stray wisps of hair behind her ears and looked miffed. If only he had some imagination. "I'm telling you, Lawrence, the Russian mob has taken over. Remember that tow truck guy, Lukov, down on Third Avenue? He's being charged with running the biggest chop shop in the tri-state area. I guess no one thinks twice if they see a tow truck driving off with a car or two."

Lawrence shook his head. "I don't know how you know such things."

"It says it right here," she said, pulling a

paper out of a pile and pointing to a small item on the front page, "that a mobster is turning state's evidence and Lukov will probably be charged with more serious crimes as well. Murder, I bet. Or kidnapping. Gangsters hide bodies in cars, you know."

"Well, I sure wouldn't want to be in the snitch's shoes. He might not live long enough to testify. Who do you think it is?"

"Could be one of Lukov's own men or a rival Russian mobster." She turned to look out the window. "Hey! Maybe it's Kobloschenko! He just drove up in a new car. Looks just like yours."

Lawrence glanced at his watch. "Hurry up, Ma. We'll be late for church."

"We're not going today. We're going up to Mercyville to cousin SarahLou's wedding. She's moved into a trailer park with her four children and she's marrying a man who has two of his own."

Lawrence hated last-minute changes. Besides, Sunday was the only chance he had to catch a glimpse of Lulu Kobloschenko taking a walk with her boy. He never actually spoke to her, though sometimes she'd smile and he'd smile back. He'd planned to say something about it being a nice day and they could talk a bit.

There was no changing Bertie's mind. She was already at the door, wearing the blue dress and pearls she wore for every special occasion, although thick shoulder pads had gone out of fashion long ago and left her with peculiar proportions.

Lawrence wore the same black slacks and

tweed sport jacket he always wore to church -- and to funerals and weddings, including his own. "I wish you'd told me, Ma."

"A little adventure never hurt anybody, but we'd better hurry. The preacher has three weddings after theirs and can't hang around waiting for late people. I made a list, by the way."

"Of what?"

"The kids' names. They're very odd and impossible to remember. One of them is Antwana Merl. I mean, really, is that a boy or a girl?"

They walked down the steps and turned to the right, out of habit, as if they were going to church after all. That's why Lawrence wasn't surprised to see his car parked in front of the trash cans, but when he put his key in the lock, nothing happened. He jiggled it, still nothing.

"My car door won't open, Ma."

"Did you jiggle the key?"

"Of course I jiggled it."

"Look it up in the manual."

"How am I supposed to do that? The manual's in the car. I'll call the dealer tomorrow. Too bad we can't go to the wedding."

"Don't be silly, we're not missing that wedding. We're her only family except for her kids. Here's my key to the house. Run back and call the automobile club. They'll figure it out. And then call a cab and tell them to hurry."

He did as he was told and they were on their way before Kobloschenko came out of his house wearing sunglasses and a hooded sweatshirt. He looked both ways before jumping into his car, tires screeching as he sped away.

Lawrence and Bertie's cab ride to Mercyville was uneventful. The wedding, on the other hand, was a painful affair. SarahLou looked haggard. Her two eldest barely spoke, while the two youngest sneezed repeatedly and wiped runny noses on already stained shirtsleeves. The bridegroom's kids kept their hands in their pockets and refused to talk at all. The bridegroom promised to look for a house in town the minute he got a job, but what with the economy being what it was, there wasn't an abundance of opportunities. The reception fare consisted of trail mix and beer -- the economy being what it was.

Lawrence suffered, but Bertie, in her usual way, made the best of it. By the time their cab showed up to take them back, Lawrence was exhausted. He didn't open his eyes until Bertie dug her elbow into his ribs and shrieked, "LOOK AT MY STREET!"

There it was, covered with broken glass, pieces of charred metal, and chunks of gray, molten plastic. A jacket that Lawrence had left in the back seat of his car lay draped over Kobloschenko's untrimmed hedge, one of its sleeves burnt to the elbow. A fire truck was leaving, and three police cars were parked at odd angles to block traffic.

"What in the world happened?" Bertie said as she reached for the door handle.

Lawrence jumped out of the cab and rushed to the nearest police car, leaving his mother to pay the fare. "Officer, I think my car's been stolen. It was parked right there on that street," Lawrence said.

"Your name?"

"Lawrence Grundle."

"I was about to call you. How is it that your car was there, Mr. Grundle?"

"My mother lives ..."

"At number 427," Bertie chimed in, a bit out of breath. "My son comes every Sunday morning."

"So, you've been here all day, Mr. Grundle?"

"No, we had to go to a wedding. Just got back. We had to take a cab because I couldn't get the car door open. The key didn't work, so I called the automobile club. It's very annoying because it'll cost me an arm and a leg, and all we had was a bunch of ill-bred kids, beer and a bowl of trail mix."

The police officer listened patiently, trying to decipher whether Lawrence's explanation was deceitful or just annoyingly filled with irrelevant information.

"How well do you know Mr. Kobloschenko?"

"I don't."

"Why were you parked in front of his house?"

"I wasn't. Oh!" Lawrence mulled over this realization as he paced. "That's why my key didn't work. You see, my mother had put her trash cans in my space so I parked in Mr. Kobloschenko's."

The officer bit his lip as he reconstructed the morning's happenings in his mind, then looked intently at Lawrence. "Do you have any enemies, Mr. Grundle? Or any grievances against anyone?"

"Enemies? No, not unless you consider the world as a whole."

"Which seems to give my son cause to have grievances all the time," Bertie added, "though I don't think they're directed toward anyone in particular, unless you count his boss' secretary, who does sound totally incompetent."

"Listen, Officer," Lawrence broke in. "Is there any chance I'll get my car back? My mother was just telling me about that tow-truck guy... what was his name, Ma? Maybe he stole it. It would be my lousy luck."

The officer put his hand on Lawrence's arm. "Good luck, Mr. Grundle. Very good luck."

"How do you figure that?"

"Kobloschenko was going to testify against Lukov tomorrow. Because you parked in his space and he in yours, someone mistook your car for his this morning and rigged it with explosives that would go off the moment he unlocked the door."

"I knew it!" Bertie burst out.

"So if I had ..." Lawrence began, ignoring her.

"You would have been blown to bits, Mr. Grundle."

"So Kobloschenko was instead?"

"No, because, at some point after you left, Kobloschenko drove off in his car, the one you had mistaken for yours."

"Then what happened to mine?"

"They blew yours up instead!" Bertie said, strangely gleeful.

"Who did?" Lawrence asked, still confused. "The automobile club wouldn't have done that."

"No, but their locksmith was unavailable so the driver called for a tow truck," the officer said.

"Lukov!" Bertie cried. "I knew it! I told you Kobloschenko was the snitch."

"That's right," the officer said. "When Lukov got the call to pick up your car, he recognized the name of the street, and apparently saw an opportunity to view Kobloschenko's remains for himself, thinking the dirty deed he had ordered had already happened. Not realizing that the car he'd been asked to tow was the one that had mistakenly been rigged, he proceeded to load the car onto his truck. The explosives were activated and he was killed."

"And Kobloschenko?"

"We heard he and his wife boarded a private plane to Cuba. With no trial, we don't expect them back."

Bertie looked disappointed.

"I thought you said a little adventure never hurt anyone," said Lawrence.

She shrugged. "I got more than I bargained for."

***

The Missing Heiress

by Deborah Owen
CEO Creative Writing Institute

Old lines draped his forty-something face as Fizz took a long drag off a short cigarette and slouched in the kitchen chair. He leafed through the newspaper and lingered at one article. "Belinda, look! This dame looks just like you." He stabbed the picture with his index finger.

Twenty-two year old Belinda grabbed a quick look as she cleared the table. "Wow. She does. Who is she?"

"Amanda Huntington, granddaughter of Bertha Huntington."

"The old bat that owns half of Sacramento?"
"The same."

"Wow. I can't believe how much we look alike. Let me see that."

Missing Heiress
Bertha Huntington of Huntington Catsup Company offers a $100,000 reward for information leading to the safe return of her missing granddaughter. Amanda was last seen at the Martindale Mall on this date two years ago.

If you have information on Amanda's whereabouts or if you have seen her, contact our office on the number below and we will forward the information to Ms. Huntington.

"You look enough like her to *be* her," Fizz

said. "You could knock on the old bat's door and live like a queen for the rest of your life."

"Get serious," she said.

"Ya know, it could actually work."

"No, thanks. I don't wanna be locked up in a mansion with an old woman for however long it takes her to die. No way."

Fizz sat up straight and downed a slug of coffee. "But just s'pose you did. The old woman is a billionaire. Would it be so bad to dress fine, have a chauffeur drive you around in a Rolls Royce, and eat the finest food?"

"Maybe I could fool her at first," Amanda said, clattering dishes, "but how would I know what the real Amanda eats, how she talks and walks, how she dresses, her favorite hobbies and heaps of other things?"

Fizz lit up. "The last time I was in the joint, I went to the library a few times. I read an article about the old woman. She disowned her daughter when she got pregnant and never had anything to do with her after that. The daughter died last year. I'm guessin' the old bat doesn't even know her granddaughter, let alone all her traits. I'm tellin' ya, you can do this. I've got an idea. I'll call the newspaper and tell 'em I know where you are. Yeah. That'll work. Grandma will cough up the hundred grand and that'll take care of me for a month or two."

"A month or two?" she said with a shout. "I could live on that for years. And if you get any ideas of offin' the ole lady, count me out."

Fizz's chair flipped over backwards as he jumped up, grabbed her black hair and slammed her into a wall. "Watch your lip or I'll bust it," he said with one fist in the air. "You'll do what I tell ya, hear me? And when the old bag is dead, we'll live in that big fancy mansion. Just think of it. We'll be wealthy for life."

Belinda pulled away, plopped onto a kitchen chair and studied Amanda's picture. "She's beautiful. I'm not."

"That's yer low self-esteem talkin'. You could be pretty if ya fixed yourself up."

"Gee, thanks."

Fizz laid a gentle hand on her arm. "C'mon, baby. You can do this, and it's not like you'll be miserable or it'll take that long. The old battle-axe has cancer. She knows she's gonna die and all she wants is her missing granddaughter. You'd be helpin' 'er, see? Look on it as fulfillin' her dyin' wish," Fizz said.

"How? By feeding her lies and false hopes? By deceiving her and stealing everything she's worked for all her life?"

Fizz leaned back, ground his cigarette out and blew smoke through his nose. "What can I say, Babe? It's a dog eat dog world and this is a once in a lifetime chance. I got it all figured out. Yer gonna do this fer your old man."

"But I don't want …"

Riveting eyes stopped her mid-sentence. Stringy brown hair hung to his shoulders and surrounded a beak nose that ruined an otherwise handsome face. Fizz slammed his open palm on the table and Belinda jumped like she was shot. "The discussion's over, doll." He reached for his wallet and unfolded some green stuff. "Here's a few bucks," he said, tossing $300 on the table. "I can give up a little booze if I know it's goin' for a good cause. Get yerself some new clothes and shoes. Cut about a foot'a your hair off so it'll look like Amanda's."

"I don't wanna cut my hair."

"Did I ask if you wanted to cut your hair? Did I?" he said with a sharp slap to her face.

She held her face and looked down. "No."

"If I wanna know what ya want, I'll ask."

"You said we were broke! I've been cutting down on food so you'd have plenty to eat and you've been holding out on me?"

"Shut yer face," he said as he fell into a chair. "You needed to lose a little off yer hiney anyway."

Belinda walked over to the hall mirror and examined herself. Raven black hair nearly reached her waist. With a cut and a little make-up, she could easily pass for Amanda Huntington, but could she fool the grandmother and the people who knew the heiress? Belinda straightened her shoulders and smoothed the blue blouse that missed a button. New clothes would be nice. At the very least, it would be an adventure – and she would be free of Fizz for a while. If she played her cards right, maybe forever.

Spending $300 on the morrow was fast, easy and fun. When Belinda walked out of Samantha's

Salon, she looked the part. When she waltzed into the dingy apartment, she modeled for Fizz.

"Heyyy, look at you, doll," he said. "Not bad. Not bad at all. Straighten your shoulders. Now walk across the room and let me have a good look."

Belinda walked back and forth.

"No, no, no! Don't walk like a prostitute on the make, ya bimbo. Walk like this — like a dainty little nun that's bored out'a her tree. Try it again. Yeah. That's better. Yeah. You got it. Real smooooth. You look downright dignified. I do believe it's time to call that newspaper. For the next coupl'a days, I'm just gonna call ya Amanda so ya get used to answerin' to it. Dig? Keep yer thinkin' cap on. And from now on, talk like a proper lady."

A week later, Belinda's plane landed in Sacramento. She shivered when she spied the chauffeur at the gate holding a sign that read AMANDA. It would be good to get away from the crowd. At least half a dozen people identified her from the ad in the paper. She straightened her body, gulped hard and walked toward the chauffeur.

"Miss Amanda, I presume," he said. "I'm Jenkins, at your service, Ma'am. If you'd like to wait in the car, I'll get your luggage."

"Yeah. Cool. I mean... thank you. How long have you worked for my grandmother?"

"Only a few months, Miss."

"Right. I didn't think you looked familiar," she said. "Is she waiting for me? I mean, at the mansi… um… house?"

"Yes, Ma'am. The maid will help you get

settled before you meet at tea time."

"Tea? Oh, right. Tea. I can't wait to see her."

"And she, you."

"Huh? Oh. Right. Sorry. I just got out of the hospital and I'm still kind'a woozy-headed."

Belinda struggled to pull her blood pressure down as they traveled. Why did she let Fizz talk her into this? Probably because she wasn't a fan of broken bones.

The mansion sat on a 100-acre plot of land, surrounded by mammoth maple trees that housed secrets of bygone days. A ten car garage? Stables? Amanda craned her neck to catch the sights as they pulled through the iron gate. A three-story house with eight gables smiled at her.

When Jenkins rang the doorbell, a little maid answered, grinned from ear to ear, and squatted in a sloppy curtsy.

"Hello, Miss. I'm delighted to see yer 'ome safe and sound," she said in a Cockney accent.

"Thank you."

They stood eyeing one another.

"Uh, would you show me to my room, please?" Belinda said.

The maid giggled. "It's still in the same place it's always been," she said with a smile.

Jenkins lumbered in beneath a load of luggage.

"Where would you like your luggage, Miss?"

"In my room," Belinda said, eyeing the maid with determination. "The maid will show you the way."

"Come along, Mr. Jenkins," the petite maid said, unruffled. "This way."

Belinda followed the troupe upstairs and into a beautiful room that sat on the southwest corner overlooking the gardens. A four-poster canopied bed swam in pink netting and glittering sequins. Belinda's heart rose to her throat. What was Amanda like? Mean? Sweet? Spoiled? She must be sweet or the maid wouldn't like her. Pawing through the room would provide clues.

Finally alone, Belinda collapsed on the bed and turned her attention to the sequins that dazzled in the netting… but they weren't sequins. Rhinestones? No… diamonds! Belinda gasped, pulled half a dozen loose and examined them carefully. Definitely diamonds. She held them up to the light. Grade-A quality, too. If Fizz could only see these. She crawled around the bed, pulling them off the netting as quickly as possible. There must be jewelry, too. Where? Why hadn't she thought of this before? She could hock the junk and fly to South America. No, France. She had always wanted to see the Eiffel Tower.

An armoire sat by the bed. With fumbling fingers and a rapid heartbeat, Belinda opened the drawers and gasped. Diamond necklaces. Earrings. Bracelets bedecked with precious stones. Custom rings in abundance. She laughed out loud. All she needed was a little time. There must be more. What else could she hock?

Belinda opened the closet door and covered her mouth with both hands. Mink stoles. Fur coats.

Evening gowns galore. And there hung the gown of her dreams. She pulled the navy satin dress out of the closet, glided a hand over the cool material and held it in front of her as she sashayed to the mirror. The scooped neck plunged deep and long thin sleeves fastened at the wrist. A tight wrap around skirt flared at the bottom. She stared at herself in the mirror. Was that really her? Beautiful? Smiling?

"This Amanda chick has good taste," she said to her image.

Enchanted, she shed her jeans and top and slipped the gown on. It fit. A gaudy diamond necklace, matching bracelet and two rings topped the outfit off. She turned to face herself in the mirror, turned sideways and pulled her stomach in. Being a fine lady might not be so bad after all. She would take her time peddling the jewelry.

A knock sounded on her door. "Missy?"

"Come in."

"Madam 'untington requests you join 'er in the study," the maid said. "Oh, Missy. You are stunning."

Belinda blushed. "Thank you."

"Just wait 'til Madam sees you!"

"Tell her I'll be down as soon as I change."

"Oh, no. Don't change. Madam likes it when you dress for tea."

"But this is a ballroom gown."

"Yes, Ma'am, and it's your grandmother's favorite dress. She'll be pleased that yer wearing it for 'er."

"Well, if you think so. I don't suppose I have

time to change anyway. Please zip me up."

The heavy satin skirt swished on the steps as Belinda descended. She felt like a proper lady. With a stomach full of butterflies, she squared her shoulders, straightened her back and swallowed hard. It was now or never. She would either fool the old lady or end up in prison for trying to do so. She entered the study, practicing her best stride.

The aged woman wore a kind but tired face, rose to meet her and opened her arms for a warm embrace. Belinda glided into those arms and returned the warm hug. Anything to stall that first eye-clenching moment when Ms. Huntington would or would not believe she was the missing heiress, but something in that hug weakened Belinda's knees. They held that position for a long moment before either pulled back.

"Let me see you. How beautiful you are," Ms. Huntington said as she touched Belinda's cheek with the back of her hand. Tears brimmed in the old woman's eyes.

"I'm so happy to be home," Amanda said, somewhat surprised at how easily the lies flowed.

"Yes. Thank God someone saw the ad and recognized you. He said something about your being in an accident and that you had amnesia. Is that right? Tell me all about it. I've been worried out of my mind."

"Umm, I don't remember much. I got a bad bump on the head. Memories are creeping back in, but the doctor said it will take time."

"Of course, of course. Don't push yourself,

dear. Let the bad memories stay lost and just keep the good ones," Grandmother said with a smile.

"That's good advice. I'll try to do that."

Belinda retired early that evening, confident she could play her role to the hilt. But what if the real Amanda returned? If that happened and Fizz heard about it...

Weeks passed and Belinda grew into her role like an actress born for the part. Fizz couldn't get to her unless he did it in broad daylight since security followed her everywhere. Other than feeling a bit smothered, it was an ideal situation.

Minor setbacks erupted, such as the time she ate left-handed, called her grandmother "Grandma" and asked for sugar in her tea.

"You've started taking sugar in your tea?" Ms. Huntington had said.

"Uh, only recently. It's fine without."

Cups of tea without sugar? Ugh. The bitterness stayed with her until the next meal. That was bad enough, but having tea twice a day was even worse.

Belinda avoided the old woman as much as possible, but marveled at her fortitude and graciousness. Cancer may have changed her pallor, but not her courage. Sometimes she sat in thoughtful silence staring into the fireplace and Belinda wondered who was fooling who.

On a cold, rainy Friday afternoon, the maid knocked at her door. "Missy? May I come in?"

"Certainly," Belinda said.

"I 'ave something for you, Miss, but you

mustn't tell a soul. It seems to be a pow'rful secret."
She handed a note to Belinda.

"What's this?"

"I don't know. A man gave Jenkins $200 to carry this note ta you, but Jenkins bein' the bashful man 'e is, asked if I would deliver it… and 'e gave me $50 for me trouble. Wasn't that nice'a 'im?"

"Yes, it was. A note? From …?"

"I don't know, Miss. It ain't none'a me business. I'd best be goin' now."

"Oh, by the way," Belinda said, "I hear footsteps upstairs, directly over my room. Who lives up there?"

The maid's color drained. "No one, Miss. It must be mice."

"I'm sure I hear someone pacing back and forth."

"I wouldn't be knowin' nothin' 'bout that, Miss. I 'ave to get back to me work now."

As the door closed, Belinda heard floorboards squeak overhead but dismissed it in favor of the note in her hand. She slapped one hand over her mouth as she read it.

Money has run out. It's time to give her a nudge. Meet me at South Bay Plaza at 3 p.m. Friday. Be there! No excuses. If you bring the cops, yer dead.

Friday! That's the day after tomorrow, Belinda thought. *Fizz is gonna make me kill Grams, and if I don't, he'll kill both of us.* She fell on the bed and cried herself to sleep.

The following morning, Belinda picked at her breakfast. Grams had one of those silent stares going… the kind that whispered love and something else at the same time, but what was the something else?

"You don't look like you slept well," the old lady said.

"No. I didn't."

"Something on your mind? Anything you want to talk about?"

Belinda cast her eyes downward lest a neon sign reel across her forehead saying, I AM A FRAUD. "Grams, I need to talk to you."

"Haven't you noticed, dear? We are talking."

"Seriously. Can we talk in the study?"

"Yes, we can do that. I think you're finally ripe," Grams said.

"I'm ripe?" Belinda's brow wrinkled.

Grams grinned. "You go ahead and I'll meet you in fifteen minutes."

"Yes, Ma'am."

"And would you do me a favor?"

"Of course. Anything."

"Wear the navy satin dress I like so well, and take your hair down and let it hang straight."

Belinda wore a puzzled look. "Alright. If you like. I'll have to hurry, but I won't be late. I promise."

Belinda arrived one minute early and paced the floor, pursued by the blue gown's swishing with every step. Trails of mascara grew as she waited for Mrs. Huntington.

Grandmother entered and took one look at the wet, red eyes.

"Here, here now. What's this all about?"

"Oh, Grams. I have so much to tell you and you're going to hate me."

"Don't be so dramatic, dear. No such thing will happen. You know I love you."

"What?"

"I said you're being dramatic, dear."

"No, the other part."

"I said I love you," Grams said in her matter-of-fact tone, picking up her knitting.

"No one has ever said that to me."

"What? That you're dramatic?" The old lady's grin was mischievous.

"No. Not that. No one has ever said they love me, and no matter what happens, I want you to know I love you, too. Remember that in the days ahead, will you? Promise me you'll remember that."

"I assure you, I will never forget it as long as I live," Grams said, staring her in the eye, "... and quite possibly throughout all eternity as well. Now tell me what's on your mind."

"I have reason to believe someone is going to make an attempt on your life."

"Well, they'll have to hurry or cancer will beat them to it."

"Grams, I'm serious. I don't know exactly when or how, but someone will ..."

"You mean Fizz?"

Belinda jumped to her feet. "You... know about Fizz?"

"Did you think I'd let a total stranger walk into my life and not check her out?" Grams said as she dropped a stitch.

"Total... stranger?"

"Yes, that's what I said. Do you see that pull cord over there? Ring for the butler, please."

Belinda spoke as she crossed the room and pulled the cord. "Fizz sent me a note. He wants me to meet him tomorrow."

"Yes, I know all about that, but thank you for telling me. I knew you would. Don't worry your pretty little head about it. Everything is under control. I have set a little trap for Mr. Fizz. He'll be going away for a very long time," Grams said, pulling out the last row of knits and pearls.

"But you have no proof. He'll get off scot-free. He always does. He has contacts in high places."

"My dear, when you live to be my age, you learn a few things, like how to expose a good-for-nothing punk. His past is about to catch up with him. He killed his old girlfriend, you know. Her name was Julianna Bigelow. And as for contacts, I doubt that his are as high as mine."

"Oh, my gosh! Can you prove it?"

"Of course. When I play cards, I don't bluff."

"But I was part of the scheme to kill you," Belinda said. "And my name isn't ..."

A knock sounded at the study door.

"Ah. That would be the butler," Grams said. "You don't have dentures, do you, dear? Now see, I'm getting old or I would have asked that earlier."

"Dentures?" Belinda said with a curious stare. "Dentures? I'm only twenty-two. No, I don't. Why would you ask that?"

"Because you might swallow them when you open that door. Now be a good girl and answer it, please."

Belinda rose on unsteady pins and opened the door, only to find herself looking into a mirror, but when she moved her hand, the mirror image didn't move with her.

The image smiled. "Hi, Sis," it said. "I've waited a long time to say that."

Voices faded to black as curtains pulled around her. A sharp pain to her head. Darkness. A gagging smell. Smelling salts. Curious heads looked down on her.

"Are you quite alright?" Grams said, patting her cheek.

"I... I think so. What happened?"

"You fainted. Do you feel like sitting up?"

"Yes." Belinda struggled for balance as she came to a sitting position.

"Now don't swoon on me again, child, but I'd like to introduce you to someone." A figure in a navy satin dress came into vision. "Belinda, meet your identical twin, Amanda."

"Twin? I have a twin? Amanda? You knew all along?"

A smiling mirror image walked around the sofa and into view.

"I'll try not to scare you to death this time. Welcome home, Sis," Amanda said with a smile that lit the entire room.

Belinda touched Amanda's cheek. "You...

you're real."

"Of course."

"But how …?"

Grams smiled at the two lovely figures sitting side by side, dressed alike for the first time in their lives.

"Oh, my. It's going to be very difficult to tell you two apart," she said. "I anticipated everything but that."

Amanda grinned. "Gramma cooked this whole thing up to find you."

"I don't understand."

"I didn't know I was a twin until a few weeks ago," Amanda said. "When you and I were born, our parents weren't married and Gramma disowned our mother."

Belinda looked at Grams, who nodded and said, "Yes, much to my chagrin, that's true. Please forgive me. It's too late to make it up to your mother, but I can make it up to you."

"Our father threatened to expose the whole sordid affair and ruin the family name," Amanda continued. "To keep him quiet, Mother kept me and gave you to him. She didn't know he would sell you to the highest bidder."

"But, my parents died in a car accident when I was five," Belinda said. "Dad's sister raised me. I ran away when I was thirteen, and …"

"And you have a rap sheet as long as your arm," Grams said. "I do my homework well. The people you call your parents are the ones who bought you on the black market."

"What made you want to find me?"

"When I learned I had cancer, I decided to bring you girls together," Grams said. "It was the least I could do, considering the mess I made of things."

"Gramma said someone had to know you, and since we're identical twins, someone was bound to bite on the reward money."

"But the ad said Amanda was missing. Where has she been all this time?" Belinda said.

"Pacing the floor, directly overhead, dying to meet you," Amanda said.

"So, that was you!" Belinda turned to her grandmother. "But how did you learn about Fizz?"

"I had the newspaper trace incoming calls, and when you first arrived, a detective dusted your belongings for fingerprints. The newspaper traced the phone number back to Fizz and the detective found his prints on your phone. Mr. Fizz has been under surveillance ever since."

"But if you knew I was a fraud and you knew about Fizz, why didn't you expose me when I first arrived?"

Grams smiled. "We were waiting for the Huntington blood to come out in you."

"You took a big gamble."

"I don't think so," Grams said. "You came through with shining colors. Forgive me for putting you through your paces, dear. And now you can put all the diamonds back on the pink netting around your bed," she said with a wink.

"You knew about that?"

"Of course. There are very few things I don't know, child."

Belinda turned to Amanda. "I apologize for stealing your diamonds and jewelry. I was going to hock them to get away from Fizz. I guess you can have your beautiful bedroom back now."

Grams laughed. "You've been living in your own bedroom the whole time. Amanda's is the next door down. You stole your own diamonds and your own jewelry! And now it's nearly tea time. You girls have time to freshen up."

Belinda wiped wet eyes. "When Fizz made me come here, I thought getting away from him was too good to be true, but I got more than I bargained for."

"You certainly did, dear."

Belinda hesitated and bit her bottom lip. "Grams, I feel selfish asking for anything at all, but I do have one request."

"Just name it, Granddaughter."

"Please, may I have sugar in my tea?"

***

BIO: Deborah Owen is the CEO and founder of Creative Writing Institute. CWI provides a variety of writing courses with personal tutors and is a 501(c)3 nonprofit charity that offers free writing courses to cancer survivors. Deborah won Honorable Mention over 16,000 entries in a Writer's Digest short story contest. She loves God, her family and Kettle's potato chips.

Legacy

by Jianna Higgins
Judge & Award Winning Author

"To my granddaughter, Abbey Louisa Nicholls, I leave my pocket watch. To my devoted housekeeper, Mary Johnson, I leave my antique vase collection. To my chauffeur, Robert ..."

Abbey sat up and frowned at the elderly lawyer in the crisp, pin striped suit. "Excuse me, what? I'm his only living relative and he left me a pocket watch?"

The lawyer adjusted his rimless glasses and ran his finger back up the document. "Yes, Miss Nicholls, that's correct. Now if I may continue."

Abbey zoned out. Maybe she'd hoped to inherit enough to pay off the mortgage and set up college funds for her three daughters. But no, clearly the man could hold a grudge. The pressure on her to produce a male heir had weighed like concrete pillars from the day she'd understood the scorn in his eyes. When people around her stood to leave, she followed them toward the door.

"Miss Nicholls, I have the pocket watch for you."

She glanced over her shoulder. "Keep it. He and I were done years ago." Her eyes widened when the object on the desk behind the lawyer shot sparks of gold into the air as if the sun glinted off its surface. Abbey gaped at the implacable lawyer in disbelief. She shot a look out the window to the dark grey clouds amassed outside, and then focused back on the watch. Nothing. It looked like it needed a clean a hundred years ago. She rubbed her eyes and remembered that she'd been woken twice during the night by her youngest child.

The weather matched her mood as she drove home, still rattled. When she pulled into her driveway, small droplets of rain pattered onto the car. After a quick dash from the garage, she unlocked her back door and reached for the coffee press. Her grandfather still pushed her buttons, even from the grave. Coffee always helped. An unfamiliar black velvet bag sat in front of the silver kettle. Pulling open the strings, she found the ancient gold pocket watch.

"What?" She threw it onto the counter as if it had burned her fingers, and she scoured the room as if the archaic lawyer was ready to jump out at her. When her fingers curled around the small bag, she realized that something else was inside. She retrieved a card in brushed gold with words printed in black calligraphy.

Go back in time to find what you need.
Your legacy awaits and you will be freed.

The other side of the card was blank.

She wrinkled her nose. "Yeah, right," she said. "I wish I could go back. There's a lot I'd change, old man. And I'd start with you." With a fresh brew to melt her stress, she sat at the dining room table and stared at the face of the watch. The outer circle had a large dial and the numbers ranged from one to a hundred. Around the inner circle, numbers only went up to ten.

That is the weirdest watch I've ever seen, she thought. "Go back in time to find what you need. What on earth does that mean?" she said to the empty kitchen. "But let's see what you'll do." She turned the larger dial to the number ten and laughed.

The moment she lifted her hand away, she spun in a whirlpool. Her body distorted, as if a thousand hands pushed and pulled at her. The pain shot daggers through Abbey, but her scream stuck in her throat. And then she was pieced back together and dropped unceremoniously onto a concrete path, outside, on her face.

"Ow," she groaned. She felt lightheaded and disoriented but pushed herself up onto one arm and touched her forehead. Her fingers were tipped with blood. When she turned her hand over, an engagement ring with a two caret princess-cut whopper stopped her breath.

"Abbey, what happened? Did you trip?"

Startled, she looked up into the concerned face of her husband's best friend. "Mark, where am I?" The sun shone too bright and she winced.

"You were carrying the washing basket to the clothes line and you fell. That's a nasty scrape on your temple. Come inside and lie down for a bit."

An unfamiliar two-story house towered over her. "Um, where's Callum?" She couldn't remember where she was supposed to be or how to get home to her husband and children.

"He and Jenny have gone on a camping holiday around the South Island, remember?"

That made no sense. Cheating on her? "Why is Callum with Jenny?"

Mark laughed but his forehead crinkled. "Jenny, his wife. You know, your best friend." He supported her to stand with an arm across her back. "You sure hit your head hard. I think you might need to see a doctor."

A psychiatrist more like, she thought. *I'm inside a nightmare where everything's wrong.* A drum beat against her brain as he helped her inside the house. Her bare feet sank into the soft white carpet and she lowered herself onto a white leather recliner. The room screamed *minimalist* and *no dirt allowed*.

"Where are my children?" She jumped to her feet but wobbled and grabbed Mark's arms. "Where are the girls? They should be home by now."

Mark's eyes clouded with concern. "Right, that's it. We're going to the hospital to get you checked out. We don't have any children, remember? You know why."

Mark always said he never wanted children. They were *small, messy little things*. If she could just see Callum, he would confirm that *he* was her husband, not Mark. She patted her back pocket. "Mark, where's my cell phone? I can't find it."

He pointed to a small black and silver slide phone on the coffee table. "Right where you always leave it."

What? I had that phone ten years ago, but in the

gold version. Was this a sick joke they were playing on her? But Mark looked younger, just like he had when they'd first met.

"Abbey, hospital."

She swallowed. "Wait. Where's the bathroom? I feel sick."

Mark pointed. "Altered memory and nausea after a knock to the head are bad signs." He followed her and leaned against the door frame.

She gaped into the bathroom mirror and stared at her 22-year-old self. She had dropped right into a cliché. How many stories had she read about time travel and rolled her eyes? Not cool. "How did this happen, you know, us getting married?"

He frowned and then shrugged. "It was my natural charm. I knew you liked both of us when we met at the Night Life bar. I always thought you'd choose Callum. But no, it was me that got lucky. Come on, let's go."

"No, I don't feel sick anymore. I just want to wash my face. I'll be fine. I know who you are, don't I?"

Mark seemed placated and left her in the bathroom. A moment later the fridge rattled as it opened.

Abbey ran her hands down over her jeans, and from the front pocket she pulled out the old watch. When she tried to turn the dial, her heart sank when it wouldn't budge. She checked her other pocket and found the gold card. It showed a different message.

Your past has lead you down this track

Now there is no going back.

What? Rules can't just change like that. Ice snaked down her spine. She touched a finger to the stunning rings on her left hand and longed for the simple gold band that Callum had placed there on their wedding day. Not only had she gone back in time, but she'd fallen into a different reality. She *had* liked both men. Mark was tall with his Danish mother's blonde hair and high cheek bones. Callum, the quiet one, had shoulder length brown hair and sparkling green eyes. It was Callum's kindness and sense of humor that had won her heart. So what had happened in this reality? She'd chosen the handsome blonde because he had three older brothers who'd all produced sons?

She swallowed hard to contain the rising nausea and marched out to the kitchen. "I have to talk to Callum. There's been a big mistake." The hurt in his eyes seared her stomach. This wasn't his fault. In her reality, she'd hooked up Mark and Jenny, and they'd married two years later. After eight years, Jenny and Mark were still childless. *How can I be married to Mark now, when I love Callum?*

Mark sighed and stared at the floor. "He texted this morning that they were heading through Arthur's Pass so they won't have cell phone coverage."

Digging her nails hard into her palms didn't help. It hurt, which meant that however clichéd, this was her new reality. With a desperate need for fresh air, she pulled open a sliding door and stood on the deck. The Sky Tower and the Auckland Harbor were easily visible, so this property was well above sea level. Ponsonby? She vaguely knew the area, but right now the only thing familiar was the blue sky.

A small whimper caught Abbey's attention. She stepped off the deck and followed the sound to the neighbor's property. Tied to a metal railing on the porch, a miniature Schnauzer puppy wagged its tail as she approached. She picked him up.

He licked her chin and snuggled against her warmth. A metal tag said *Shelby*.

She leaned against the wall and slid down onto her bottom. This baby was too little to be left outside alone. No wonder he cried. And then she visualized her daughters as babies and how she'd hugged them to her. To never see them again squeezed her throat, and her eyes brimmed.

Suddenly the front door yanked open and a large man towered over her. "I wondered why the mutt had stopped that infernal racket." A scowl matched his hard eyes.

Abbey backed up against the railing. "Shelby's just a baby. He's scared out here all by himself."

The man snorted. "Take it, if you care so much. All it does is whine. Don't know for the life of me why I got it. They all think they're smarter than me." He scratched at the spiky shadow on his face with nicotine-stained fingers, moved down to the exposed belly that hung over his jeans, and then reached behind to scratch his backside.

Abbey pushed herself to her feet and jumped straight off the side of the porch. "Sure. I'll take good care of him." And then she remembered. Mark loathed children *and* dogs. Too bad. She entered through the back door and held up the puppy. "Look what the neighbor just gave me."

Mark looked up from a book, genuinely distressed. "No, no and no. Take it outside." He pointed to the door. "Tomorrow you can drop it at the SPCA."

All her negative feelings about men… being ignored, bullied and abandoned, boiled up and spilled over. "This is my *baby*. You won't give me one, so either Shelby stays, or we both leave. You choose."

Mark looked at her as if she was an alien, but his face softened. "Shelby, huh? Well, if it means that much to you, just don't let it come in the house with dirty feet." His eyes raked the pristine white carpet even though Shelby had not left her arms.

As she walked away, she called over her shoulder, "Shelby is a *he,* and he's the only son you'll ever get, so be nice to him." She wandered through all the rooms and finally found her bedroom. The nightie under the closest pillow suggested that was her side of the bed. Lifting the shiny silk comforter, she slipped under it and closed her eyes. Maybe she'd wake up from this nightmare and be back in her own house with Callum and the girls. The longing for them ripped at her guts and silent tears rolled down her cheeks.

Shelby snuggled into the crook of Abbey's arm.

The smell of fresh coffee and the sound of a

cup plunked on the bedside table forced her eyelids open.

Mark beamed at her. "I was getting worried. You slept 16 hours. How do you feel?"

How do I feel? I want to go home to my family. Back to the moment before I turned the dial on that pocket watch. Or back to just before my grandfather died so I can ask him how he could hate me so much. "I feel fine, thanks Mark."

After a plate of steaming pancakes with strawberries, the walls pressed in on her and she had to get out. On a small wall rack, two car keys hung side by side. She presumed one car was hers. "I think I'll go for a drive and get a few things for Shelby." But which car?

"Take the beamer, babe. Can you fill it up? It's running on fumes."

She reached for the keys with a BMW logo attached to the ring and scooped up the puppy. Once she found College Hill and hit the motorway, she was oriented. As she drove north across the Auckland Harbor Bridge, she looked at the sparkling water below and felt numb. Fifteen minutes later, the car screeched to a halt outside the home she shared with Callum. Although the trees and the plants in the barked gardens looked unfamiliar, she didn't pause. Pulling open the back door, she called, "Callum, girls, where are you?"

A strange woman stood at the kitchen sink drying dishes. "What do you want? Who're you looking for?"

"Where's my husband, Callum, and my three

daughters? We live here. What're you doing in my house?"

The woman grabbed a large knife from the bench and held it in front of her. "Look, I don't know who you are, but I live here with *my* family, not you. Now get out before I call the cops."

Abbey drove, unaware of her location, and then discovered she'd parked outside her grandfather's house. A housekeeper with small eyes and sour expression showed her into the library. The air smelled of roasted coffee and cigar smoke. She'd always hated the ominous dark walls and mahogany bookshelves. There was enough room for two of her in the creaky old leather chair.

He finally made an appearance, leaning heavily on his silver tipped cane. "When are you going to give me a grandson? And where's that husband of yours?" His mouth looked like an upside down U.

She wanted to say *which husband?* "He's at home, busy." Why had she come? Could she ask about the watch?

"If you give me a boy, I'll leave all my money to him."

She stood, fists clenched and her rage ignited. "You will *not*. If I had a son, he'd have three sisters. I'm not going to let you make them feel like they were never good enough, the way you always made me and my mom feel."

"What're you talking about, girl? You don't have any children. You've only been married six months." His eyes lowered to her flat stomach and he sighed.

She leaned close into his face. "Well, I'm planning on having at least three daughters. And they and their fictitious brother will have nothing to do with you. Keep your money. Give it all to charity. I don't care. Just don't leave it to me or any of my children." The object in her pocket felt warm against her leg. "Or your stupid watch. I want *nothing* from you."

As she started the car, she realized she didn't know the way back to Mark's house. Her house. In an instant, a thought slammed into her brain. *Mom.* Ten years ago, she had been diagnosed with cancer but still alive. She pulled out the slide phone and dialed the number she remembered. Disconnected beeps pulsed in her ear. After a search in the phone's contacts section, she pushed the green symbol.

"Yes, hello?"

The familiarity of this greeting warmed her soul and her lip trembled. This woman had been gone from her life for the past nine years. Now she was alive again. This added to the weirdness but added a small dollop of awesome. "Mom, it's Abbey."

"Abbey? How lovely. Are you going to come and see me?"

Should she play the concussion card? How else to explain her missing information. "Yes, but I don't know where you live." If the phone number she remembered was wrong, there was a good chance her mother didn't live at the family home in

Brown's Bay.

"Oh, of course. You haven't been to visit me since I moved into Stuart's house."

What? "Stuart?"

"Your stepfather. The one I married a few months ago. Are you all right, honey? You sound a little strange."

As she drove back along the motorway, the brisk air whipped her hair into a frenzy. It helped still the frenetic thoughts in her brain. Before she had reached the door of the hacienda-style house, it swung open.

"Darling," her mother wrapped wiry arms around her. "It's so good to see you."

Tears sprang into her eyes. It had been so long. But she'd regained a mother and lost a husband and three daughters. Guilt seeped through her because if she had to choose, she wouldn't be here. She shook off the emotion. "It sounds like you haven't seen me for ages." As they moved inside, she glanced at an oval frame on the stereo cabinet and recognized her mother in a pale pink gown, but not the man in the black tux.

"Three months is a long time not to see or hear from your only child. I know you aren't thrilled about Stuart, but he's healed a lot of my pain."

Abbey lowered herself onto a stuffed, floral couch. That was a loaded statement. Pain caused by cancer or pain caused by men? And three months without seeing her mother. Who was she in this reality? A selfish little twerp who ignored her mother and married for the wrong reason? In her own time, they had talked daily and she'd visited at least twice a week. "I'm sorry. I'm glad you have someone special to take care of you for these last few months of your life."

Her mother's hand fluttered in front of her face. "My last few months? You make it sound as if I'm dying. My doctor said after my checkup last week that I'm healthy as a horse."

Not dying of cancer? Oh wow. "Um, I meant someone to take care of you the last three months while I was… still getting used to being married myself."

"How is that husband of yours? Changed his mind about giving me a grandchild?"

Clearly her mother knew of Marks dislike of children. "No, but we got a puppy today. He's in the car and his name's Shelby. He'll have to do." *For all of us.*

After a lot of subtle questions and news of extended family, Abbey checked her watch. "I need to get to the pet store before it closes, Mom, but I promise I'll be back tomorrow."

"Before you go, I have a little gift for my new grandson." She left the room for a moment and returned carrying a thin, blue, diamond studded collar. "I bought this for my little Maxi, but he passed on before I had a chance to give it to him. It's brand new."

Abbey had no idea if Maxi was a dog or a cat, or even a parakeet. "Thanks, Mom, it's great. I'm sure Shelby will love it." There was still the issue of her address. "Mom, how do I get home from here?"

She parked outside Animates pet store, and gathered food, bedding and other items in a daze. In this reality, she had a healthy mother. When she had died, something had broken inside Abbey and never fully mended. And then there was Shelby. The small puppy had already crept into her heart. As for Mark, they were good friends. If this was now her future, she'd eventually get used to it, but the loss of her daughters burned through her soul and she knew it would never stop hurting.

Dark had settled when she pulled into the driveway. She lifted out the puppy and his paraphernalia and carried them inside. A smell of garlic-flavored spaghetti sauce greeted her. She'd forgotten how much Mark liked to cook. She settled Shelby and made small talk as they ate.

Two hours later, Mark stood and stretched. "Come on, let's have an early night."

Major glitch. She hadn't thought about the going to bed part and what married couples did before sleep.

She lay, unengaged, as Mark kissed her. *Callum, I'm so sorry. What've I done to us? Our daughters will never be born.* That was unimaginable. Blond haired Nicole with her father's green eyes and sunny smile. Golden haired Krystal with a mischievous grin and thick black lashes that framed her blue eyes. Dark haired Cassie with yellow-ringed blue eyes and whose laugh was a magnet to anyone nearby. The thought of them never even existing dropped rocks into her stomach. Small tears trickled down the side of her face as she violated her marriage vows.

Weeks passed, and each day blurred into the next. Visiting her mother with Shelby became a daily event. Mark flew to Wellington on business for two days every week but phoned at night. With the puppy in her arms, it was easy to play her part and say the right words to him.

One afternoon, Abbey sat curled up next to her mother on the couch. She wondered about telling her mother what had happened. With caffeine surging through her veins and lemon cake consumed, she said, "Tell me about Grandpa. Why is he so mean?"

Her mother's hands shook as she set her cup on the small table. "He was crushed when I was born a girl because your gran couldn't have any more children. My whole life he behaved as if I didn't exist. When you were born and your father left not long after, I swore off men."

"Is that why you never dated?"

"Oh yes. I had no interest in having more men in my life. My grandfather died when I was little. He was hateful to women, but he doted on my father. It's been generational that only male heirs are of any use. I worried that I'd passed my negativity onto you, but you and Mark seem to be okay."

"And Stuart?"

"Ah, he fought hard to break down my walls. Eventually I realized that not all men are emotionally distant like the males in my family, or a runner like your father. "

Abbey sat up straight and her shoulders

tensed. A light bulb flashed in her mind. Her mother's negativity *had* affected her feelings toward men. Since the day she'd married Callum, she'd expected him to abuse her or to cut and run. Her behavior toward him had mirrored her feelings. How had he put up with her for ten years? Had he stayed for the children? That was now a moot point. The thought of moving forward with this new knowledge almost helped.

Her mother continued. "Mark's a good man, though. You got one of the few good ones."

"And Callum, you know him, right?"

"Mark's friend. Yes, he was best man at your wedding. He seemed nice, too. His wife's your best friend, isn't she? Lucky girl."

Callum, I didn't know what I had until I lost you. I love you so much. If I'd been happy with what I had, this wouldn't have happened. As she formed her next question to her mother, she felt the pocket watch heat up against her leg. She reached in and pulled out the card. The words had changed again.

This watch took you backward, you've learned something true.

Now you will start your future anew.

This time, the message shot a warm glow through her heart. Bright white light whipped around her head and down to her feet, and she felt herself falling through space. Then there was nothing.

A monitor beeped, a trolley rattled on rickety wheels, people whispered, and Abbey opened her eyes. "What happened? Where am I?" A plastic mattress crackled beneath her as she shifted her weight. Then she saw Callum, biting his knuckle. She was back? She checked her wedding ring and almost cried in relief, but she said a silent goodbye to her mother.

A young nurse touched her hand. "You're at the hospital. You fainted so the doctor ordered some tests. Congratulations. You're going to have a baby."

She froze. "What?" *No. I can't have Mark's baby.*

"You've had an ultrasound scan to ensure the baby's okay. You're having a boy." The young woman's eyes widened and her cheeks flamed. "Woops. I think I was supposed to ask if you wanted to know." She hurried from the cubicle.

Callum moved closer and sat on the side of the bed. "Did you hear? We're having a little boy. The girls will be so excited."

Nausea surged through her stomach at the wrongness. Could she ever tell him it wasn't his? Instead, she attacked. "You always wanted a boy, didn't you?"

Callum winced. "No. If we only had the three girls I would've been perfectly happy. If this baby was another girl, I would be just as ecstatic. The baby's gender makes no difference to me, just that you and I made him together."

Abbey rubbed her eyes. He looked genuine. "Okay. Let's go." she said. "I have to see the girls." As Callum pushed her wheelchair to the doors, adrenaline surged through her body. *What happens when this little life inside me grows up tall and blonde, the image of his daddy's best friend?*

Once home, she cuddled with her daughters until she couldn't keep her eyes open. "Mommy's going to have a quick lie down, okay," she said. "Look after Daddy." As she walked to her bedroom, the card in her pocket vibrated. She pulled it out.

Contact the lawyer.

Unsurprised at the changed words, she leaned against the pillows and dialed the number after the words. When a gruff voice answered she said, "It's Abbey Nicholls."

"Your grandfather left you a message."

She wanted to say, *so what?* "Aha?"

"You're welcome."

"What? You haven't told me the message yet, and I highly doubt that I'll be thanking you."

"That *was* the message."

"He told me I was welcome? I underestimated his arrogance. Look, I have nothing to say to you, so …"

"Your grandfather and I were good friends for a long time and I knew about the watch. I didn't believe him at first, but I saw the change in him." When he received no response, he coughed and continued. "He used it a few weeks before he died. Said he had a long discussion with his own grandfather and learned exactly why happiness had evaded him. He didn't want that for you and your children."

"Why didn't he call me?"

"He thought you wouldn't take his call. Was

he right?"

"Yes."

"There you go. He left you everything that wasn't bequeathed to his staff. You were the only person who stood up to him and rejected his money. He was truly impressed."

She rolled her eyes. "Why couldn't you have said that when you read the will? Aren't you legally obligated to be open and transparent?"

"I was just following instructions, Miss Nicholls."

With gritted teeth she said, "Well, I don't want his money, and I could never live in that monstrosity he owned."

"He knew you'd say that. But he also knew that you'd find a use for them."

Her finger traced a swirl on the bed's duvet cover. "I guess his mansion would be a great halfway house for women trying to escape abusive partners. And yes, the money could help so many different charities." The girls would get their college funds after all. She touched her belly. Her son would also go to college, and life would be easier thanks to the old man. Her anger toward her grandfather evaporated. He'd wanted a male to carry on his name. She could help out with that.

Then next day while Callum was at work and the children at school, Abbey drove back to the house she'd lived in with Mark and stared up at the house, now painted pale blue. A small movement to her right caught her eye and she looked across to the neighbor's property. A dark grey Schnauzer on the concrete porch had stood to stretch and then settled back to sleep. She edged out of the car and walked across the grass to get a closer look. It couldn't be. She swallowed and whispered, "Shelby?"

His head whipped up and around and then he bounded toward her. His whimper sounded both excited and distraught at the same time. He leapt into her arms.

"It's really you? But how?" His muzzle had turned grey but his eyes still sparkled.

She knocked on the front door, uncertain of what to expect. Or who. Mark didn't live next door unless this reality had changed as well.

The door creaked as an elderly woman opened it in slow motion and peered over her glasses. "Yes?"

"I was just wondering about your dog. I, um, met him several years ago."

"Is that right? Well I've had Shelby ten years and all he does is sit on that deck as if he's waiting for his real owner to show up. Some gratitude, eh?"

Abbey scratched the top of his silky head. "I think he was waiting for *me*."

"You go ahead and take him then. He never gave me one ounce of affection. Little blighter looks quite at home in your arms."

Abbey carried Shelby to the car and set him on the seat beside her. And then she noticed the faded blue, diamond studded collar. The same collar her mother had placed on Shelby in that altered reality. The name tag looked a little worn, but it was also the same. Shelby and the baby had come forward in time with her. *What about Mom? Could she still be alive?* Her shoulders slumped when she checked her phone contacts and her mother's name was absent.

She drove home and her three daughters *oohed* and *aahed* over Shelby. Callum said nothing, but his grin told her he was okay with this new addition to the family. While the girls and the dog played, she moved closer to her husband. "Do you mind if we call our son William Adamson Nicholls?"

"After the old man?" He studied his knuckles for a moment. "Sure, why not?" When the phone jangled, Callum answered it. He said, "Mmhmm, sure, yep," and put down the receiver. "Jenny and Mark are on their way over to celebrate the baby."

Oh, no, please no. She couldn't celebrate this new baby when it was really Mark's. Not yet. She tried to swallow, but her throat was too dry. "Celebrate?"

Shelby jumped onto Callum's lap and he ran a hand down his back. "Yeah. Did Jenny tell you that she and Mark have been approved to adopt?"

Abbey blinked. "I thought Mark didn't like children."

"Mark's never liked what he can't have."

She drew in a sharp breath. "What do you mean?"

"Mark can't have children. I thought you knew. He had chemo as a kid and it um, wiped him out."

Already pregnant. Callum's baby. She sagged into a chair. With relief came a flood of emotions. She felt a sense of peace at what she had learned, the affirmation of her love for her husband, Callum, and gratitude for all of the blessings in her life. She patted the watch in her pocket and whispered into Shelby's ear, "When I turned the dial on my grandfather's watch I got to spend time with my mom, I let go a whole stack of grudges, and I got you. I got more than I bargained for." She kissed the top of his silky head and smiled.

***

BIO: Jianna is the author of the *Sorrento* series and she is currently working on the *Silver Sleuth* series. Her books have won two Gold Medals and an Honorable Mention medal in the Global Ebook awards, and they have been finalists in several novel contests, including Readers' Favorite, the Kindle Best Indie Book Awards, and the Writers' Village International Novel Contest.

Jianna loves her family, chocolate, supporting the All Blacks rugby team and sliding on snow.

http://jiannahiggins.com/

The Secret Cave

by S. Joan Popek
CWI Staff and Award Winning Author

A quiet place. That's all Kate needed, just a place to be alone. A place away from the prying women and pity stares of the men. A place where she didn't have to explain why she didn't cry when she sat holding his hand in the ambulance with its blaring siren, why she didn't cry when she sat in the stark white hospital room huddled in the corner with a thin blanket the nurse had given her, why she didn't cry when they lowered her husband's coffin into the cold, wet earth.

Then later at the gathering at her house, she sat quiet and relaxed as the minister and others tried to comfort her with platitudes and tired expressions that meant nothing.

Eventually, each person turned to the festive table laden with food to stuff their mouths with rich treats and drink the free wine and liquor. While feeling good about comforting the poor widow, they discussed the day's events with each other.

She stood, glanced around the room and quietly escaped out the front door.

No one noticed her leave.

The air smells good, she thought. A fresh breeze brought the scent of lilacs from the bush in the front yard to caress her senses. She breathed deeply and stepped off the porch. The freshly cut grass released its fragrance beneath her shoes. She smiled and kicked off her dress shoes to feel the grass between her toes. "Ahh, I never did like those stupid shoes anyway." She wiggled her toes and the grass gently tickled her feet.

She turned to the side of the garden and picked a lilac bloom as she passed the bushes. Her feet took her where she wanted to go even though, right now, she wasn't sure where she wanted to be. Sniffing the lilac, she stopped in front of the grape arbor. "Oh yes, the secret cave. That's where I need to be." She stepped into the arbor, which was neither a secret nor a cave to anyone else, and closed her eyes.

The odor of freshly turned earth brought flashes of days gone past that flitted through her mind. She smiled as she envisioned herself and her husband digging the trenches for their coveted grape arbor. Then she saw the kids laughing and running in and out as they played hide and seek and gathered ripe, juicy, red grapes for the table. Other images of this place played in her mind like an old movie she had seen many times. But the one that stuck was the day her husband named it *The Secret Cave*. She smiled as she remembered.

It was a warm, summer evening many years ago. He had found her sitting on the bench at the very back of the arbor. "Are you hiding, honey?" He laughed and dropped down next to her. "Can't say I blame you. The kids asked if they could bathe the dog. I said yes, but I got more than I bargained for. Not a pretty sight." He chuckled, reached for her hand and said, "This is our secret cave."

The memory made her laugh aloud. Today, she sat on that same bench and closed her eyes.

"Hello, honey."

She opened her eyes, startled. "Charles?" He stood in front of her just as he had so many years ago. "But... but how are you here? I just came from your funeral. How are you ...?"

"I'll always be with you, honey. You know that." He moved to sit next to her on the bench. "You're remembering when the kids were young and we used to hide here, right?"

She smiled and relaxed. *This can't be real, but I don't care. I don't care.* "Yes." She nodded as she felt his warm body next to her, his strong arm across her shoulder. His musky, aftershave scent made her heart pound.

"Honey, you must let me go. I don't want to leave you, but I must. You know that."

She looked at his dear face next to her. "No I can't. I just can't. What about the kids, the life we planned? What about ...?"

"Honey, the kids are grown. Tom and Andy have families of their own and Carrie is in her second year of college. You're still young enough to do many of the things we planned. Don't let my death stop you from living." His warm hand grazed her cheek lovingly. "Remember me, mourn me, cry for me, then live your life. You must do this for me."

"I- I can't. I can't cry for you. If I cry for you,

it'll mean you're truly gone. I can't bear that. I just can't."

"Of course you can, my love. You must. You must go on for me as well as for yourself." He stood up and pulled her up to him. Wrapping his arms around her, he whispered, "See the Sphinx for me. See the Alps for me and all the other things we planned. Do it for me and for you."

"Oh, Charles, I don't know if I can exist without you." She tried to hug him back, but her arms wouldn't move.

He pulled away gently and held her at arm's length. "I must go now."

"No!"

"Yes, I must go. And you must mourn. Cry your grief out, and let me go so we'll both have peace. If you hold it in, you'll be bitter and tired. You mustn't do that. You must be free."

He stepped further back. "I'll always love you."

She screamed, "No... no." But he was gone and she knew it was forever. She slumped back on the seat and stared into the empty shadows.

"Mom? Mom? Are you in here?" Her daughter Carrie's worried voice sounded from the opening of the arbor.

Kate looked up, "Yes, yes, I'm here."

Carrie hurried to her. "I was so worried when I couldn't find you. Then I remembered the secret cave and hoped you were here."

"Secret... you knew we called it that?"

"Of course. All three of us kids knew."

Carrie laughed. "We just didn't tell you 'cause we knew it was supposed to be a secret." She hugged Kate. "Hence the name, Secret Cave."

Kate smiled and said, "Carrie, you're on break from college next month, right? How would you like to see the Sphinx?"

"Oh, Mom, I'd love it."

Kate smiled, brushed an imaginary wisp of hair behind her daughter's ear and said, "Good, it's a date."

Carrie jumped up. "Great, I'm going to tell Tom and Andy. They'll be so jealous." She grabbed her mother's hand. "Come on, let's go tell them."

"You go ahead. I'll be in soon."

"Okay. I know Dad would be happy we're going. I miss him so much."

"Me, too, sweetheart. Me too." She watched her daughter thread her way out of the grape arbor and head to the house. Smiling, she smelled the lilac bloom again, sat back down on the bench, then at last, she wept.

***

BIO: S. Joan Popek was owner and editor of Millennium Science Fiction & Fantasy Magazine and The Roswell Literary Review. She also wrote a monthly column called Ask Dr. WEB-Write for Millennium. She has been published in over 250 fiction, nonfiction and poetry works in various magazines. Her book, The Administrator won the 2000 EPPIE Award, and her nonfiction book, Jumpstart Your Career With Electronic Publishing, was a 2002 EPPIE Finalist.

Maybe Next Time

by L. Edward Carroll
Short Story Contest Judge and CWI Tutor

At some point, for those of us who have wandered off, we all feel the urge to gather the loose ends of family ties and make an effort to weave and stitch them together again. A career in the military, having separated me from my brothers and sister, I decided to start knitting up old ties and re-bond with my favorite brother, two years younger than myself.

As kids, Fred and I were inseparable. We shared a rich imagination and engaged in so many dare-devil adventures that our parents had serious doubts about ever procreating again. I have to admit, I've often marveled at how we survived our harebrained stunts, like parachuting off the garage roof with ropes tied to the corners of a bed sheet, or shooting arrows straight up into the air and running for cover.

Mom always said, "Because of you two knuckleheads, old doc Campbell's going to retire a rich man."

Sadly, as teen-agers, Fred and I grew apart, and as adults we lived in different states… sometimes in different countries. We seldom saw or talked to each other until the coming of the internet.

Reconnecting via email, I decided to drive up

from North Carolina to visit him and his Peruvian wife, Cholie, in New Jersey. Cholie had dropped some heavy hints that he needed help with a long-neglected home remodeling project. For me, an amateur cabinet maker, it presented the perfect opportunity to rekindle memories with my brother.

After an uneventful drive up I-95, Fred greeted my wife and I with a big smile. With his ham-sized hand stuck way out there, he looked like an older, overweight Hulk Hogan with the same white Fu Man Chu moustache. Standing next to him, I felt like an older, overweight Peter Parker, (the alter-ego of Spider Man).

After handshakes and bear hugs, we headed straight for the kitchen table and popped cans of cold brews as I scanned the bare wall-studs with embedded cabled wires and plumbing.

"How long do you think it'll take us to finish this, Fred?"

Before he could answer, Cholie said, "How you like my skeleton house? For ten years have I been looking at this." She waved her hand at the forest of two-by-fours. "Even in my village in Peru, we had walls. Please, brother, maybe can you help him to finish my walls this weekend?"

Across the table, Fred shrugged and gave me a look that told me what he'd been putting up with for a decade.

"Sure, no problem, sis. That's why I came to visit."

Ten years ago, when Fred decided to remodel his kitchen, he removed the old plaster down to the bricks and mortar, and erected the necessary two-by-four studs for the new walls and doorways. Somewhere along the way, the living room got involved. Although it turned into a major renovation, everything was coming along splendidly. With the wall-studs erected and the electrical wiring and new plumbing completed, all that remained was to install the drywall and paint it. However, for some reason, and I'm sure the shrinks would have a field day figuring that out, the project ground to a halt. For a decade or more, the kitchen and dining room walls, along with his wife, waited for the project to be completed. Their two boys were raised amongst a forest of wall studs, and they thought it was neat to walk through walls instead of using doors.

Me? I was beginning to think I got more than I bargained for.

His wife, bless her stoic Peruvian soul, was expectant, yet not fully confident that she would ever see her new walls, but I was determined her wish would come true that weekend.

While our wives took the Amtrak into the Big Apple to go shopping, we sat at the kitchen table, and, between runs to the refrigerator and the second floor bathroom, held a strategy meeting.

"I'm thinking we'll need fourteen sheets of drywall," Fred said.

"You can't do it that way," I said. "First, we have to measure."

"Whaddaya mean?" He leaned his head back and long-throated a sixteen-ounce can of Miller

High Life, then crushed the can. After a loud belch, he said, "How many houses have you built?"

"None," I said, crushing my empty can right back at him, "but you can't guess at it. If you're not going to do it right, why do it at all?"

"Aw, John," he said popping another can of beer, "you're full of it." He let out another long, loud belch, and the aroma wafted across the kitchen table. His eyes were slits under overbearing white, bushy eyebrows.

"If you don't wanna help me, just say so."

"Just humor me on this," I said. "Where's your tape measure?"

"I don't know. I don't think I even have one. I told you, we need fourteen sheets of drywall and we'll put it up this weekend."

"Can't we borrow one from a neighbor?" I said.

"Borrow what?"

"A tape measure."

"I'm not talking to any of those buttheads."

Across the table, Fred looked at me and made a tent with his hands. Sitting there with his great beer belly, he reminded me of a Buddha statue with a Fu Man Chu moustache.

"I told you," he said slowly and with all the patience one reserves for a thick-headed child, "we need fourteen sheets of drywall, but if you wanna measure it, be my guest. Anyway, it's late and we might as well forget it today. We'll get a fresh start in the morning. What'cha say we go get another case of beer?"

He was right. It was too late to order the drywall delivery, but instead of calling Home Depot with the order, we walked the two blocks to Crowley's Bar, crossing sidewalks cracked by harsh winters and buckled by relentless tree roots.

That evening, when our wives returned from the big city, they found two philosopher-kings sitting at the kitchen table, awash in empty beer cans and cigarette butts. It was obvious that no drywall had been installed. No sir, but all of the world's problems had been solved. They held their noses and went upstairs.

Saturday morning, accompanied by a world class hangover, I drove myself to Home Depot and bought a tape measure. As I measured for the drywall, I could hear the nasal honky-tonk twang of Hank Williams accompanied by scratchy clicks of a dull needle on an ancient dust-coated LP record. Fred was already into the Millers.

Determined to stay focused, I finished measuring the walls and placed an order for fourteen sheets of drywall (who knew?), a bucket of screws, drywall tape and mud.

That afternoon, our supplies arrived closer to five o'clock than noon, as promised. We directed the deliverymen to stack the sheets of drywall neatly in the back yard. Fred played Hank Williams and Johnny Cash records and then started on the bagpipe music as we worked our way through another case of Miller's. We decided that since the walls had already waited ten years, another day wouldn't hurt. Due to the delays, my wife and I decided to stay another day or two to finish the project.

Sunday morning found our carefully laid plans dashed. It had rained hard and steady all night. I can't imagine how we could have slept through all that, but there you are. As a result, the once neat stack of drywall boards sat in a soggy mess in the middle of a small lake that had formed overnight.

With the call for more bad weather, we had to return to North Carolina. I best remember Fred standing at his front door, beer in hand, towering over Cholie.

"Goodbye, my brother," he said. "Next time we'll come down to North Carolina."

I looked at Fred and then at Cholie. "Sorry I couldn't be more help this time. We'll be back soon and finish the job."

She gave me a one-sided grin and shrugged her shoulders. "Whatever," she said, smiling.

Fred's big friendly face beamed. "Yeah. Next time."

"Yeah, we'll finish it for sure," I said.

That was two years ago. Today, Cholie's home is no longer a skeleton house. When Fred died of a massive coronary, she had a professional come in and finish the walls.

Well, they finally got done.

***

BIO: L. Edward Carroll is a graduate of Long Ridge Writers Group, The Institute of Children's Literature, and is a former writing tutor at A-1 Writing Academy. He also has a background as a Computer Systems Analyst, has an Economics major, and is a former entrepreneur. Born and raised in Greenfield, Massachusetts, this ex-Marine drill sergeant now devotes himself to drilling fledgling writers at Creative Writing Institute.

The Book

by Emily-Jane Hills Orford
CWI staff and Short Story Contest Judge

"I got more than I bargained for," I announced as Claire sat quietly staring into her almost empty tea cup. "I really did. Now everyone's going to be mad at me. You, too."

Claire looked up at me warily. She took a minute to raise her cup to her lips and drain the remaining tea, then she asked, "What do you mean."

I fidgeted. "Well, first of all, there are a few things you need to know." I paused briefly to let my words sink in. 'Few' was a very vague term. There were probably more than a 'few' things I should disclose, but a few would suffice for now. At least, I hoped it would.

Claire looked at me askance. She eyed me cautiously from across the table. Her long, pink painted nails clicked repetitively against the china surface of the empty cup. The clicking jiggled the cup which clattered against its saucer. It was annoying, but that was Claire. Her deep, dark eyes looked at me with impatience, as she quickly, almost mindlessly, flicked a strand of her long, blonde hair back off her face with a mere twist of the neck. It was subtle, very seductive; it was something she had mastered years ago. For me, though, she was being nothing but annoying. She knew it, too. She took pleasure in that simple fact. Why wouldn't she? I was just her annoying little sister.

"What!" It was neither a question nor a statement, just a word. She snarled it impatiently. Did I mention that Claire was not one to demonstrate patience? She never had been; why start now?

I squirmed uneasily in my seat. I was never very good at making ultimatums, nor was I good at making confessions. I wasn't quite sure that I was making either, but I lunged ahead anyway. That's what Claire would expect of me, to blunder on aimlessly until I finally reached the point, whatever that was. It was a game of chance that we had played since childhood. Claire, the older sister, beautiful in every aspect, perfect in all that mattered; me the baby of the family, pampered, only pretty in a minor sense, shy to a fault, certainly not the officious, effervescent personality of the older sibling.

"I am not what you think I am." I blurted it out with as much panache as I could muster. It fell flat, of course. Outshined by my glorious sister, everything I did or said in her presence always fell flat.

Claire laughed a cold, heartless laugh. "So, who is?"

"I'm a writer," I stated blankly.

"I think I already know that," she retorted with a weak laugh. "So what? You write pulp fiction. Big deal! Are you rich?"

I shook my head. "No," I admitted. "Far

from it. It is my livelihood, I'll admit, but it's not the main reason why I chose to be a writer. I write because I have to write. That is my focus in life. That is my purpose. That is my means of communication. I never was a talker, always out-talked by the rest of the family."

"Yeah, right!" Claire mimicked wiping a teary eye. "Out with the violins. So what's the big deal?"

"I wrote our family's story," I said, looking her square in the eye.

Claire flinched. "I'll sue you."

I shook my head again. "Your name doesn't appear in the story. I changed everyone's names."

"But my friends will know it's me," she pointed out.

"Only if they read," I said.

"They read," she snapped defensively, clicking her nails more rapidly against the china tea cup. "I think."

"Do you?" I asked. "Do you read?"

"The paper," she confessed. "Sometimes. I read my emails. I read messages on Facebook."

"Not the same thing," I chuckled lamely. "I was careful what I wrote. It's actually Mom's story. I wrote it from Mom's point of view. The family just happened to be a part of Mom's story." I shrugged self-consciously and looked my sister square in the eye, daring her to challenge me further. I blundered on aimlessly trying to defend my actions, protect my book. "Read it and you'll see for yourself. You can't stop it from being published. It's already gone to print. It's been reviewed and I'm going on live radio later this week to promote the book. You can try to sue. It will only bring out the worst in both you and our family story. Plus, it'll help promote my book and make it sell faster. Your choice."

I stood up abruptly, pulling my coat off the back of the chair. "That's it?" she snarled. She was good at snarling. "That's your big news? That's what I needed to know? You said there were a 'few' things I needed to know. You only mentioned the book."

"You asked me if I would, if I could, put you up for a few months," I noted. "You want to stay with me, to live in my space, then you have to know who I am and what I've done. A 'few' things are a list of things that affect my writing life. I write most mornings, early until noon. I don't like interruptions and I don't like complaints about what I write and what I do in my space in my time. If you can't live with that, if you can't live with me, the real me, the writer who is exposing our family's story, then you'll have to ask one of your reader-less friends to help you out." I shrugged into my coat.

"Wait!" she called, stalling me again from a hasty exit. "Okay. I get it. Write. Publish. Hang out our laundry, dirty, clean, whatever." Her shoulders sagged in defeat, her nails ceased clicking. "I'm not mad at you. I won't sue. Don't have the money for a lawyer anyway. When can I move in?"

Now I was certain that I got more than I bargained for!

***

BIO: Emily-Jane Hills Orford has pursued

her passion for writing stories about the 'real' people in her life. She has published several books, creative nonfiction stories mostly about her family. Her award-winning novel, *F-Stop: A Life in Pictures* (Baico 2011), is her mother's story. It was named Finalist and received the Silver Medal in the 2012 Next Generation Indie Book Awards.

http://emilyjanebooks.ca

Cotter Castle

by Ernie Lindsey
USA Today Bestselling Author

Every Sunday for the last forty-one years, Herman Cotter promised his wife that *today* was the day he would begin working on her castle. Cotter's wife would smile, shake her head, and roll her eyes when his head once again disappeared behind the morning paper. She would refill his coffee mug, ask if he'd prefer bacon or sausage with his eggs, then set about her day.

There were dishes to wash, floors to sweep, and shelves to dust. She would check in from time to time, just to see if he truly would head out to that sagging old barn, with its graying wooden slats and rusted door hinges, and drag out his tools.

It never happened.

Which was fine, now that hope had become habit.

She'd heard a quote once, and it didn't matter who said it or when, because the words meant just as much today as they did when the person said them.

There are three keys to happiness: someone to love, something to do, and something to hope for.

She had Herman. She had her chores that kept her hands nimble and her resolve strong. And she held on to the slightest flicker of hope for that doggone castle.

On their wedding day, midsummer 1974, he had lifted her veil and smiled with gratitude. "Beautiful. You look like royalty," he'd whispered. "And one day, I'll build a castle for my queen."

Like many young girls, she had dreamed of such things. Glamorous gowns, white gloves, stately horses—they were all part of the mirage that included a majestic castle, high on a green hill, overlooking a sloping valley lush with a thick forest, a flowing creek, and magical creatures dancing under the moonlight.

As he slid the ring on her finger, and she became Mrs. Herman Cotter, she had her king, the man who would build it.

Instead, what she got was a two-story farmhouse with white siding and black shutters, situated on twenty acres of land in southwest Virginia, nestled in the rolling Appalachians. Cotter reminded her that while the house wasn't quite what she had dreamed of, the land would be the perfect spot to build high walls made of stone.

She agreed. Eventually.

The boys came first, a year apart. Cotter's wife scrubbed the floors on her hands and knees between changing cloth diapers, tracking down baseball gloves, and cooking hot meals. There were toothaches and sore throats, blue jeans that needed patching, haircuts with dull scissors. First cars and first loves. High school graduations and the cost of two college educations.

Promises were made each Sunday morning, but no castle.

Then came Cotter's mother, who stayed silent and stoic in her corner rocking chair. Eyes blue and vacant. There were more diapers to change. Soft food was served on spoons that had lost their shine. There were daily injections. There was yellow laundry that smelled of stale urine. There were earplugs to dull the noise when things got worse. There was a quiet spot, out behind the dilapidated tool shed, where she could breathe and have a moment on her own. Hospital visits, home nurses, and the cost of a flowery funeral.

But no castle.

She often convinced herself that the palace would never come. Maybe she knew it all along. Maybe the realization had always existed as a pinprick of simmering lava inside her chest, and one day it finally erupted, demanding attention. Yet she couldn't fully let go of the hope. Cotter was a man of his word. Always had been, and that was one of the reason's she had married him. Honesty and integrity holding hands with that mischievous smile? She couldn't have resisted if she had tried.

Never fully surrendering, Cotter's wife gradually allowed acceptance and hope to trade places. Now, her dream was tucked away in some small corner of her heart, a tiny fragment that only she could feel.

She often wondered why, four decades later, he would continue to tease her with the promise. Did he hold onto the same idea—that the mere *idea* of the castle was a symbol of hopefulness?

She had her own revelation once, sometime during the Regan era, that possibly the castle was a metaphor; Cotter's way of saying it was the start of another week. A week in which he would get up, go to work at the local furniture factory, and earn a living for their family, slowly building up the walls, the ramparts, the crenellations, day by day, stone by stone.

For a while, she accepted this as the truth, and buried her disappointment in a box in the attic, along with a tiara and gown that she had worn for Halloween one year.

Then one summer afternoon, ages ago, the year after the second boy had left for good, Cotter came home with a load of rock and some cement mix. Some time after that, he bought a shovel and a shiny new trowel. A hammer with the price tag still attached showed up on the kitchen counter. Another time, a truck carrying a load of long wooden planks, supposedly for the drawbridge, unloaded them in a stack where they now sat on the eastern side of the old barn, slowly smothering in tall weeds.

So, there were signs, and Cotter's wife reopened the attic box, sometimes daydreaming about the possibilities, but never giving them room to blossom.

Cotter retired, leaving plenty of time for stone walls to rise high up on the hillside. Or so she thought.

Instead of moats and towers, she found him one afternoon planting neat, parallel rows of tiny evergreens. Acres of them. They needed nurturing and time. "Do you know how much people pay for these things during the holidays?" Cotter had asked, already knowing the answer. "You just wait. In a few years …"

And still yet, each Sunday morning, Cotter would poke his head out from behind the newspaper, insist that today was the day he would begin working on her castle, eat his bacon long after it had grown cold, and then disappear into the fields.

The trees grew tall. Sunday mornings came and went.

Once the Christmas trees were ripe for the season, Cotter put up a hand-painted sign and sold them all. He used fat rubber bands to hold the bills together. That spring, there was a used backhoe parked in the barn and Cotter's wife thought *this* could be the year.

The backhoe sat untouched. The yellow paint faded. The tires dry-rotted throughout the seasons. Rust crept into exposed corners.

Grandchildren found their way into the world. Black dresses were worn for friends who were called to a different castle in the sky.

Then, on a sunny summer Saturday, the trucks began arriving one by one, along with a massive crane that unloaded stacks upon stacks of stones, cinderblocks, and bricks. Cotter's wife threw a wet dishrag onto the kitchen counter, thrust open the screen door and marched outside, shaking a finger as she scolded him. "You're making a mess of the yard," she'd said. "I've just about had it with all this castle nonsense. You'll kill the grass."

The following morning, Cotter poked his head out from behind the newspaper. "Today's the day. I'll start working on your castle after breakfast."

Cotter's wife clenched her teeth and shoved the frying pan across the stovetop. "You've been working on that castle for forty years, and there's nothing to show for it. Nothing. All I see is a bunch of rusty junk that you've dragged in here. Or there's weeds all over it. We don't have enough time left for this nonsense."

Cotter smiled at her. "Exactly."

"Exactly what?"

He closed his newspaper and stood up from the breakfast table, gray and groaning. Hard work had left him healthy and strong for his age, but it couldn't hide the wrinkles and spots. He reminded her of a carved pumpkin that had sat outside too long, shriveled and shrunken. But he was hers, and she felt sorry for lashing out.

Cotter took her hands and kissed her on the cheek. "I've been *working* on it for forty years, my darling, now I'm finally ready to *build* it."

She sighed, grinned, and felt the warmth in his palms. "Why wait so long?"

"I wanted the best for you, and nothing ever seemed adequate because when I put that ring on your finger so many years ago, well, I got more than I bargained for."

"And so did I," she replied. "But why build it now?"

"Something occurred to me yesterday. I can make this, I can grow that, but the one thing I can't create on my own is more time. So, I figured that despite whatever reservations I might have, I better get moving before these old bones can't swing a hammer or lift a rock. Betty Cotter will have her castle."

"I don't need a *real* castle to know that you've already been my king all these years."

"I made a promise, and I intend to keep it. My queen will have her throne."

Cotter's wife giggled. She felt like she was twenty years old again. The way he raised his chin and puffed out his chest, arm held high in royal fashion, caused her to laugh harder. Silly. Cherished.

"Okay," she said, "if you insist, but we'll make it together."

"We always have."

Stone by stone, brick by brick, plank by plank, they worked.

No... they *built*.

***

BIO: Ernie Lindsey is a USA Today bestselling author of more than thirty novels and short works of fiction. A small-town farm boy and native of Virginia, Ernie currently lives with his family in the Pacific Northwest.

http://www.ernielindsey.com/

Cassandra's Legacy

by Patricia Paris
Amazon Bestselling Author

Forsaken. It was the most fitting word I could think of to describe the old, colonial-style brick house I was staring at through Shepherd, my vintage Volkswagen beetle. The place was solid. It had been built to last, but it stood abandoned, untended, and as lonely as an unwanted puppy dumped on the side of the road.

A few patchy remnants of paint curled along the wooden window frames. They fluttered in the dry breeze like dead leaves clinging futilely to a winter branch, a withering reminder of their former glory.

A jumble of overgrown roses and azaleas partially obstructed the front porch. At one time, the gardens had reflected a loving hand, but like everything else they'd been deserted, left to run as wild as the rumors surrounding my ancestral home.

Lucky for me, the cloak of superstition that had shrouded the place for more than a century served to keep would-be trespassers out. If I found squatters, I suspected they'd have four legs and furry tails.

I got out of the car and picked my way up the weed-pocked brick path. Despite the forlorn appearance, I was anxious to see inside my new home. It had been part of my great-grandmother, Cassandra Beauchamp's trust, bequeathed to her first direct female descendent who reached the age of twenty-six. Enter me, the only female born in three generations.

As I crossed the porch, my cell phone vibrated in the back pocket of my jeans. I pulled it out and looked at the screen. *Mom... probably calling to see if I was still alive.* I dashed off a quick text to let her know I'd arrived safely and would call later. It wouldn't alleviate my parents' concerns about my moving here, but at least they'd know I had phone reception and could cross that worry off their long list of objections.

I'd miss them; but I'd counted the years, then months, then weeks until my twenty-sixth birthday when I would inherit my legacy and could move into a place of my own. I wouldn't be dissuaded from following my dream because the place allegedly had a supernatural resident or two. I didn't believe in ghosts, but even if they did exist, they couldn't be much scarier than some real people I'd met.

Squinty sunshine glinted off my front window as I drove into town the next morning. Despite the glare, I enjoyed the drive. After living most of my life in the city, this diminutive town with wide open fields and yawning woods, unmarred by the bulldozers of progress, felt like another world.

I soaked in the picturesque landscape. Rows of cornstalks had turned the color of straw with the onset of fall. There was an apple orchard on my right, trees pregnant with ripe red fruit on the left, and a pasture with horses grazing in the distance.

Wanting to experience it all, I pushed the automatic control to open the windows and let the air rush into the car. I sucked it in, filling my lungs with a clean, sweet scent that was a little bit grassy, and fresher than anything I could think of. It smelled like the country, or at least my idea of what the country would smell like.

I came to a tee in the road and turned right to follow the arrow pointing to Redville. I still had to switch my driver's license from New York to Pennsylvania, reregister my car, and take care of all the legalities that would make everything official, but for all intents and purposes, Redville was now home, and I was anxious to explore my new community.

Driving through the quaint downtown, I craned my neck to read the signs on the storefronts. Spotting what I was looking for, I backed into a parking space. A few minutes later I walked into Angela's Diner, eager to get some breakfast and hopefully meet a couple of the locals.

A cluster of bells hanging on the door jangled my arrival. Inside, booths lined the street-side wall, giving customers a front row view to the goings-on in town through wide-pane windows. Opposite the booths was a long counter with chrome swivel stools, complete with red vinyl seat cushions, most of which were occupied.

Business was brisk for a Monday morning, which piqued my curiosity. Who were these people? What did they do? Were they meeting others here for business purposes or just hanging out eating pancakes and sausage?

Curious faces turned in my direction. Who was I? What was my story? I could read the questions in the eyes that followed me to the counter. It didn't offend me. I had the same questions about them, but I was the unknown in a place where everyone else probably knew each other.

I claimed a stool at the counter and glanced around, smiling at the people scrutinizing me when I made eye contact with them.

"Good morning, do you want coffee?" An efficient, fifty-something waitress stood on the other side of the counter holding a gold thermal coffee carafe with a black lid.

I nodded. "That would be great."

She flipped over my cup and filled it, then pulled three creamers from the pocket of her apron and set them next to the cup. "Do you know what you want or do you need a menu?"

I glanced at her nametag and then back at her face. "I'll have some scrambled eggs and bacon, Carla. Thanks."

"You got it, doll." She turned her head and looked over her shoulder at the lanky cook who was frying everything from potatoes to omelets on a large flat grill that took up the back wall behind the counter. "Two eggs, wreck 'em, side of bacon." Order in, she turned and worked her way down the counter, filling cups and exchanging chit-chat with customers.

"Hi," I said to the handsome man sitting to my left. He was peeling back the foil seal on a packet of jam... the ones that seem to be indigenous to diners everywhere.

He acknowledged me with an abbreviated head bob and mumbled a non-committal, "Mornin'." He was wearing a pair of faded blue jeans and a long sleeve denim shirt with the sleeves rolled up just below his elbows. The dark auburn hair hung straight, shot through with burnished red streaks, and his cheeks bore the stubble of a couple of day's growth. He had that rugged look, but if a woman liked that kind of thing, she would consider him attractive.

I wrapped my fingers around my cup and took a sip of coffee. Not to be deterred by his brevity, I turned slightly in his direction. "Is it always this busy here?"

He looked sideways at me through dark, deep-set eyes that didn't waiver a spit when I offered up a friendly smile.

"I just moved here," I said, thinking it might thaw some. "I got here yesterday, so this is my first trip into town." I put down my cup and stuck out a hand. "I'm Zoë. Zoë Beauchamp."

He didn't take my hand, or tell me his name in return, but his eyes narrowed when I said my name and I wondered if he was making a connection between me and the town's more infamous Beauchamps. I understand that being the descendent of a calculating, brutal murderer might give some people pause, but his response, or lack of one, just seemed rude.

"Did I hear you say you just moved here?"

Carla set my order on the counter, her eyes wide. "You didn't move into the old Beauchamp place out on Lake Road, did you?"

By the time I left the diner forty minutes later, I was pretty sure everyone who'd been there knew Cassandra's great-granddaughter had come to town and was intending to stay. It appeared that Redville's rumor mill was alive and well, and news of my arrival had set it on fire.

A few mornings later, I rolled onto my back and stared at the ceiling. Drip. Drip. Drip. A storm had blown in and whipped white caps on the lake behind the house. The storm lost its steam after a couple of hours and the only remnant was a light but steady rain. Rain… and an incessant drip that I now lay awake waiting for, every five seconds.

I growled in frustration, threw back the covers, and rolled out of bed. After turning on the lamp on my nightstand, I followed the sound and located the source. A droplet quavered in the middle of a growing wet spot in the corner of my bedroom ceiling, and waited to fall. *Drip.* Another one immediately formed in its place.

Great. I hadn't been here three days and I already had major repairs. I got a towel from the bathroom to soak up the water, and then went downstairs to find a pail. I found a white metal bucket under the kitchen. Based on the looks of the rusty pipes, it had been there to catch a leaking drain. *Fantastic!* Apparently I had plumbing problems, too.

You knew this was an old house when you decided to move here, Zoë. Mom told you it would have problems. Dad told you it would be a money-pit. Well, yeah, but…

I pulled the bucket out and stood up with a sigh. It didn't matter. I'd already fallen in love with the place. So what if it had a few quirks? It had a world of potential, and I loved living on the lake. I'd hiked along the rocky shoreline for a few miles the afternoon before the storm hit. I'd felt more at peace than I'd ever felt, as though coming here had been my fate. I belonged here. I don't know why I believed it so strongly, but I did, and I wouldn't let a leaky roof or old plumbing or anything else chase me away.

I turned around and froze. The bucket slid from my fingers, tumbling to the kitchen's wide oak floorboards with a clang. The woman standing in the kitchen doorway watched in silence, with a pale-blue dress that cinched at her waist and hung just above the laced-up boots. Her dark hair was twisted into a single, long, thick braid that hung down over her right shoulder and was tied off with a piece of blue silk ribbon.

My logical mind said she wasn't real. There was no leaking roof. I never got out of bed. I wasn't standing in my kitchen looking at an ethereal woman that I could see through. It was all a dream… but it felt so real.

I let out a slow breath and took a step forward. "Wh… who are you?"

Her fingers fluttered and she brought a hand to her heart. Then she faded and was gone, and I stood staring at an empty doorway.

I rubbed my eyes and slid my hands to the top of my head, linking my fingers over my skull where I held them as I tried to come to grips with what just happened. I was awake. I knew I was awake. So, who or what had I just seen? Or, had I just imagined her? It was late, after midnight, and I was tired, so maybe…

No. I hadn't imagined her. She had been there. I wasn't given to fancy, and hadn't been thinking about anything other than dealing with a pesky leak, so it wasn't like I would have just imagined her out of nowhere.

Shaking my head, I picked up the bucket and, reminded once again of the problem upstairs, walked out of the kitchen and went back to my bedroom where I had a very real drip to deal with.

It was late October and Halloween was only a few days away. Although I doubted any trick-or-treaters would venture this far out of town, I'd bought a bag of Twix minis just in case. They were one of my favorites, so if no one showed up they wouldn't go to waste.

I hadn't had any more close encounters of the unexplainable kind, which made me question if I'd really seen the otherworldly woman in my kitchen doorway. I flipped the bacon I was frying. If I had inherited a ghost for a housemate, why hadn't she made another appearance?

The doorbell rang, interrupting my train of thought. I'd called someone about the roof a few days ago and he was supposed to come out this morning. I turned off the range and went to answer the door, expecting a repairman named Seth Garrison. When I saw who stood on my porch, I frowned. "You're Seth Garrison? You're the contractor I talked to about my roof?"

"You got a problem with that?" he said. It was the man I had unsuccessfully tried to converse with at the diner. He crossed his arms and stared down at me. He was taller than I remembered. Tall and built well, but surly.

I bit back the urge to ask if he ever smiled. I needed my roof fixed and he had a truck with a big ladder on it parked in my driveway and, I assumed, stuff to stop my leak.

"No, of course not," I fibbed, and motioned for him to follow with the fork I'd been using to flip the bacon.

"It must be coming in right above this corner," I said when we stood in my bedroom a couple of minutes later, pointing out what seemed obvious.

He ran his hand over the wall and around the window frame next to the corner. "The thing with water is it travels until it finds a weak point. I won't know where it's getting in until I take a look at the roof." We walked out of the room and he asked, "What's the name of that song she's singing?"

"What song?"

He flashed me an irritated glance and then

looked down the hallway toward the end bedroom. "Someone's in that room singing a song that's stuck in my head since the day you ...." He narrowed his eyes and took to the stairs. "Forget it."

"Wait a minute. You really hear someone singing?"

"I said forget it," he bit out over his shoulder, and then stalked out of the house, not bothering to close the door.

I watched him get the ladder from his truck with brusque and angry movements. *Okay that was weird.* I rubbed my chin as I watched him. There had to be more than coincidence operating here. Were we connected somehow... to this house... to the woman I saw? The woman he heard singing?

Closing the door, I turned to go back to the kitchen and stopped short. The ghostly woman I'd seen last week stood in front of me. Seeing her again startled me, but I wasn't afraid. I sensed no malevolence in her.

"I don't know what you want," I said, more curious than anything else, "but if you need something from me to... I don't know... be at peace or whatever, maybe you could give me a clue."

This was unchartered territory. I was just warming up to the idea that ghosts were real and now I was trying to converse with one. I'd come a long way... or I'd gone crazy.

"So, that guy out there ..." I hitched my head toward the door. "It's not just a fluke he's here, is it? Or that he heard you singing? Are we linked somehow… him, me… you?"

She smiled softly.

"Those old boxes and trunks in the attic… are they yours?"

Her head dipped in a nod.

"You're related to Cassandra… to me?"

Another smile.

"And you think that man and I should be together? Well, I think he's extremely rude, and I don't like him." There was a sharp rap on the door and I turned toward it.

Seth leaned against the door frame. "Hey, look, we got off to a bad start, and I apologize for that. Will you give me a hand out here with something and then let me buy you lunch in town?" He looked over my shoulder and one corner of his mouth lifted.

I nodded, unable to find any words.

"Good, I'll meet you out by the ladder."

When I turned back, the woman had vanished. Had he seen her? If so, he obviously wasn't alarmed, as if seeing a ghost was an everyday occurrence. Maybe she had appeared to Seth and sent out silent messages? Maybe *she* was Cassandra? Was the murderer her son? Would *he* show himself at some point?

Perhaps I should have felt more cautious or fearful, but I didn't. Whatever Cassandra's reasons or the twists of fate that skipped three generations before her wishes could be carried out, the Beauchamp house and its ghosts belonged to me.

I felt a sudden, unexplainable protectiveness

for them. They'd been entrusted to me. I didn't know what that meant, or what my future role would be in all of it. I only knew one thing for sure. *I got more than I bargained for.*

As I walked out toward the ladder, I smiled. It would be interesting to see what roads fate would lead us down… and just how intertwined our lives would be.

***

BIO: Patricia Paris is an award-winning author of five full-length novels, including the bestselling contemporary romance Glebe Point Series, featuring This Time Forever, Letters to Gabriella, and Return to Glebe Point. Her romantic suspense novels include Run Rachael Run and A Murderous Game. When not writing, she spends her free time exploring the Chesapeake Bay area where she lives, battling the weeds that insist on invading her gardens, or experimenting with a new recipe in her kitchen. She is an unapologetic romantic and loves to give her readers that happily ever after, every time.

http://patriciaeparis.blogspot.com/

A Conversation

by Apryl Baker
USA Today Bestselling Author

I slipped inside the hospital chapel. Quiet
surrounded me. Chapels always seemed hushed
somehow. Most folks came for the comfort it
offered, but not me. I found it slightly funny that I
ended up here. I had no faith in God. I'd written
Him off a long time ago. No, I came to find a place
to collect my ragged thoughts and regroup. It'd been
a long morning with leaving my purse on the bus
and attending an appointment with the oncologist.

My eyes found the simple cross that adorned
the wall in front of where I sat. I snorted. I couldn't
count the number of times I'd seen people grip the
crosses they wore and pray in hopes of comfort.
Stupid people. No, the news delivered to me a few
minutes ago only reinforced my opinion on the idea
of God. Hadn't I suffered enough in this life? I was
so tired.

Stage four cancer. Who knew that a little
stomach pain would turn into cancer? Not what I
was expecting. Maybe an ulcer, but not cancer. I had
maybe six months to live. The doctor told me there
was really nothing they could do at this point. I
could do the chemo, but it might or might not help.
I didn't want to spend the last months of my life so

sick I couldn't get up and down without puking. No, I wouldn't do the chemo. Six months? Really, how much worse could it get?

I didn't want to die. I had so much left to do. My life wasn't grand, just the average, ordinary life of a regular person. I went to work, paid my bills and sometimes had a little left to indulge in a pair of Jimmy Choos. They were my favorite shoes even though I had no place to wear them. I wasn't a bad person. I did my best to stay out of trouble and I always tried to help anyone who needed it. No one had helped me, so I tried when I could to make sure others got help.

Why? Why me? I wanted to scream, to shout, but I didn't. There was no one to rail at. Just me.

"Here, Miss, I think you might need this."

I looked around, startled to see an elderly gentleman holding a Kleenex and smiling down at me with kindness in his warm blue eyes.

"Thank you," I said, and wiped my eyes. When had I started to cry?

"Are you alright?" he asked, and sat down next to me.

"I'm fine."

He arched a brow in disbelief. "You are not fine, young lady. Would you like to talk about it?"

"No," I shook my head.

He frowned, but nodded. He saw me staring at the cross. "I'm sorry. Did I interrupt your prayers?"

"No," I said with a laugh. "I don't pray."

"Then why are you in the chapel?"

"It's quiet in here and I needed someplace to think."

"You don't believe in God." A statement, not a question.

"No," I said. How could I after everything that had happened?

"That's okay," he smiled at me. "It doesn't matter if you believe in God or not."

He wasn't going to try and convince me?

"No," he continued. "All that matters is He believes in you."

I snorted. Yeah, right.

He reached over and took my hand. "It's true. God loves all of his children, even the ones who don't believe."

"If you say so."

"I do."

Stalwart old gent, I thought. He sounded so sure of himself.

"Well, thank you for the Kleenex," I told him and tried to pull my hand away. "I really need to get going."

He wouldn't let go. "You need help, young lady," he said. "Let me help you."

"There's nothing you can do," I said, a little surprised. It'd been a long time since anyone offered to help me.

"I can listen," he nodded. "Sometimes all we need is for someone to listen."

"I have cancer," I told him with a sigh, not understanding why I even told him. "I just found out this morning. Stage four. There's nothing they can do."

"Are they sure?" he asked.

"Yes."

"I will pray for you."

"That's nice of you, but ..."

"But you don't believe," he laughed.

I smiled at that laugh. It was full of warmth and happiness.

"I can see why you might not believe after receiving that kind of news," he smiled. "It would make most of us question His will."

"I haven't believed in God since I was a little girl," I told him and groaned. Why had I said that? This old man seemed to have a way of making me say things I didn't plan on.

"Why?"

I looked up into his concerned face and wanted to tell him. He reminded me of my grandfather. The old man died when I was nine. This gentleman's eyes held the same concern my Gramps had. That must be why I felt a strange compulsion to talk to him. "Because of everything," I leaned back against the pew.

"Tell me."

"My mom left us when I was five. She took my little sister, Mary, with her. She left me with Dad. He was a drunk. A mean drunk." I flinched away from the memories. "He'd get mad over the littlest things and I was too little to fight back. There were times he'd beat me so bad, I literally couldn't walk for days. I remember thinking on the way to the hospital, *would this be it? Would I finally die this time?* So, tell me, old man, where was God when Mama left me there? Where was God every time Dad took his fist to me?"

The old man's gaze never wavered. "What else happened to you?"

"I worked hard in school so I could get a scholarship. I figured it was my only chance to get out. And I did. Full paid scholarship to NYU."

"That sounds good. Things startin' to look up for you?"

"At first. Then I met Steven. He was so good to me. I'd never had anyone be so nice. I met him in February and he graduated in May. He got a job in Chicago and convinced me to go with him. Said he loved me. No one had ever loved me or treated me like he did."

"So you went?" he prompted.

"Yeah, I dropped out of school and moved to Chicago. That's when Steven started to change. Little things at first. He'd get mad when I didn't do things just so or if I criticized him in any way. He started to tell me how useless I was and how I should be grateful to him. No one else would want such a useless, lazy person. After a while I started to feel worthless and even grateful I had him. You start to really believe you are worthless. Stupid, I know. People don't understand how anyone can stay in a relationship like that. It's even hard for me to understand."

"Did you leave him?"

"Eventually," I said. "When I got pregnant, he was furious. I've never seen him like that. Sure, he'd hit me a time or two before, but he just lost it. Beat me to within an inch of my life. I lost the baby and I left him. I stole his wallet while he talked on the phone and snuck out of the hospital that night. That's how I ended up here in Virginia."

"And you still think God wasn't there?" the old man asked.

"If there was a God, then my baby wouldn't be dead, would it?" I grouched. He was causing old memories to stir and I didn't need to feel them today. I had enough to worry about. "Anyway, I've been here in Richmond for about three years. I thought things were finally starting to turn around, you know? I had a decent job, could pay my bills, and had a little extra left over. I should have known better. Cancer. They told me I have cancer."

The old man shifted so he could look at me. "God is with you, child."

"I'm not trying to knock your beliefs, sir, but I just don't believe that. Your God is supposed to be kind and merciful. All I've ever known is pain and disappointment. I used to pray, but gave up on that. If there is a God, he didn't listen to me."

The old gentleman smiled at me. "Of course he heard you. He may not have been able to stop what was happening to you, but He heard you, Jayna. He held your hand with every blow from your father's hands, and he wrapped himself around you while Steven beat you, and when your daughter died, He shielded you and protected you as best he could. He gave you the strength to leave your father. He has always been with you, Jayna, and He always will be even if you don't believe it."

His words, so gently spoken, pulled at me. He sounded so sincere that for a moment I wanted to believe him. I wanted to believe that God hadn't abandoned me. I wanted that faith I saw in so many others.

"Hush, child," he soothed and pulled me into his arms. His grip was surprisingly strong for one so old. He even smelled like my Gramps. The scent of Old Spice made me sneeze. I found myself crying. Years of pain and anger came pouring out he just held on, murmuring nonsense words to me.

"I'm sorry," I said at last, mortified I'd broken down. "I didn't mean ..."

"None of that," he said. "You needed to let it out. You'd held all that in far too long, Jayna. Don't you feel better now?"

Surprisingly, I did. Oh, the thought of dying still scared me, but I felt much calmer now and the memories he'd stirred up didn't seem quite as painful. Strange, but they didn't.

"Thank you," I pulled away from him.

"Good things are coming to you, my child. You just have to hold on, have a little faith." He stood up. "Remember what I said, Jayna, God didn't abandon you. He's here with you and always will be. All you have to do is take His hand like you did mine."

Then he was gone and I was left with my thoughts again. Could the old man be right? Could

God have suffered with me even if He couldn't have stopped it? Was that why I was sitting here today? Because he had shielded me and kept me from dying all those times at the hands of the people who were supposed to love me? I didn't know. I'd have to think about it.

Well, Jayna girl, I told myself... wait, the old man had called me Jayna. How did he know my name? I hadn't told him. Who was he? I got up and left the chapel. He'd only been gone a minute. Surely I could catch him. Instead of the old man, I found a man about my age in the corridor wearing a lab coat. He was talking to a nurse and she pointed toward the chapel. He turned and spotted me. A smile spread across his face and he said something to the nurse and then he came over to me, holding my purse.

"Hi," he said. "You left this on the bus."

"How did you ..."

"I jumped off the bus at the same stop, but you beat me inside and I couldn't find where you went."

"Have you been standing there long?" I asked him.

He shook his head. "About a minute," he said.

"Did you see where the old man went that came out of the chapel?"

His frown deepened. "No, the only person that came out was you, Miss Cross."

My eyebrows shot up when he said my name.

He gave a sheepish look. "Okay, so I checked in your purse. How else was I going to find you?" he smiled. "Besides, when you left your purse this morning, I saw my opportunity. I've been trying to get your attention for ages on the bus, but you keep your nose buried in your books and never look up."

"What?"

"So what do you say, Miss Jayna Cross, can I buy you a cup of horrible cafeteria coffee while I give you some news?"

"What news would that be?" *Good or bad?*

"I work in radiology so you were right in the next room. Then you took off and I found you here."

"So, what's the news?"

"I was the one who checked your MRI. Radiology had misread it. I recognized your name on the top and came looking for you. Someone said you'd headed toward the church."

Hope sprang to life. "I'm not dying?"

"Nope," he said with a grin. "So what do you say? Will you grab a cup of coffee with me?" He held his hand out.

The old man's words came back to me. *All you have to do is take his hand. Faith. Good things will come for you.*

My mind froze with the possibility of the impossible. It couldn't be... but no one else had come out. Could it have been? Tears welled up. Maybe He had always been there and I just hadn't let myself feel it.

Faith. Maybe that's what having faith meant. Accepting the impossible.

I could try. "I'd like that," I took his hand. "But only if you tell me your name."

His eyes widened slightly and then they settled into a smile. "Adam," he said. "My name is Adam."

Hmm... faith.

He led me to the cafeteria and we settled into an easy conversation.

That was three years ago. Standing here today looking up into Adam's smiling face as we said our wedding vows before the minister, I couldn't help but remember that day. It had forever changed my life. Good things did come to me and I thanked God every day for making me feel His presence. That day three years ago, I got more than I bargained for.

I glanced out into the audience and found the smiling blue eyes of the old man. He tipped his hat to me and then he was gone.

Faith. All it takes is a little faith.

"Thank you, God," I whispered.

*****

BIO: Apryl Baker is the USA Today Bestselling YA author of the Ghost Files, soon to become a major motion picture. She grew up in the southern mountains of West Virginia but now resides in North Carolina. She loves reading, writing, watching scary movies, and entertaining people with her stories.

http://www.aprylbaker.com/

Grandma Crazy Town

by DelSheree Gladden
USA Today Bestselling Author

I would kiss my sister full on the mouth the next time I saw her. Staring out the window of the cab at the gorgeous old apartment building, I couldn't believe how things had worked out. Four years older than me, Bernadette had always taken care of me. This was above and beyond. The moment I called her to gush about my acceptance to culinary school, she had all the answers.

Her boss had been trying to talk her into taking an overseas assignment for months, but she was still under lease. Solution: let me move in while she was in Spain. I would get super cheap rent while going to school and she wouldn't have to box everything up.

Stepping out onto the curb, I could barely keep from jumping up and down. At twenty-three, I was finally living on my own, ready to start a top notch program. It was a few years later than originally planned, but it was perfect.

I was startled out of my glorious revelry by my one, gigantic suitcase being dropped at my feet with a loud slap of plastic wheels against concrete.

"This is where you're going to live?" the cab driver asked. He looked like he was shying away from the building like it might have cooties. "I should have known when Bernadette called the cab company to pick you up at the airport."

"Isn't it great?" I said, determined not to let him ruin my moment.

"That's what everyone thinks… at first," he grumbled. "Good luck."

Having already paid him, he drove off a few seconds later. I had no idea what his problem was. I didn't have more than a second to dwell on it before a woman burst out of the building and bounded down to shake my hand. It seemed a little overenthusiastic, but I was beaming and shaking back with equal gusto.

"You must be Eliza Carlisle, Bernadette's sister, right?" The woman stared at me expectantly, looking ready to pass out from excitement. This place was really friendly. No wonder Bernadette liked it. It might take a little getting used to. I hadn't been real tight with people lately, but I was pretty sure I could manage.

"Yeah, I guess she told you I'd be here today." *Either that or she's the world's most perky stalker.*

Her smile grew, which I hadn't thought possible. "Yes, she told me all about you."

Bernadette knew how to keep her mouth shut when she needed to. It was no surprise to anyone when she went into journalism.

"I'm Sonya, the manager, and I'm here to welcome you and get you settled." She reached for my suitcase, and I thought about trying to stop her, but it seemed rude to say no. And I was a little afraid of provoking her into some kind of super welcome mode. Instead, I followed her up the steps while she continued to talk.

"I can't tell you how excited I am to have another woman my age around here. I mean," she said, looking back at me while she yanked my suitcase over another step, "your sister was really nice, but she was hardly ever around. It'll be great having someone to talk to."

I guess I hadn't really thought about how old Sonya was until that moment. She was young, but I hadn't realized she was that young.

"How old are you?" I said.

"Twenty… four," she said, her words broken up by the effort of hauling my suitcase over another tall step. "My grandma owns the building. When managing it got to be too much, she offered me a rent-free apartment in exchange for keeping an eye on things."

That explained a few things. "Sounds like a pretty good deal to me."

For the first time since meeting her, Sonya's smile faltered. "Yeah, well, it'll be better now, right?"

Not really sure how to respond to that, I nodded and hoped it was the right response. When her smile wattage went back to blinding, I figured I'd guessed correctly.

Sonya pulled one of the doors open and gestured for me to go ahead.

Stopping to stare as soon as I entered the foyer, it took me a moment to take it all in.

It was beautiful with its dark wood scrollwork and vintage wallpaper. The carpet runners were a little worn, but high quality and well cared for. It felt like home instantly.

"I closed the dumpster lids. Are you happy now!" some shuffling, grumbling older gentleman snarled as he made his way across the foyer.

I looked back at Sonya, hoping he was talking to her and not me.

She rolled her eyes, but her voice was perfectly pleasant as she said, "Thank you, Mr. Piper."

He flapped his arm a few times in annoyance without turning back and disappeared around a corner.

"Never mind him," Sonya said as she directed me to the office. "He's always like that."

She brushed it off quickly, but I tucked the warning away for later. *Avoid angry old men ranting about dumpster lids.* If Sonya and I were the only younger residents, I hoped not all the others were as irritable as Mr. Piper.

"So," Sonya said once we were both seated in her office, "let's get all the paperwork out of the way and then I'll show you to Bernadette's… well, *your* apartment, okay?"

"Sounds like a plan."

I swear it was like watching a little kid handing over a birthday present. Sonya seemed nice—a little overly so—but I couldn't for the life of me figure out why she was about to bust a seam over this. It was just a lease agreement. She pushed the paperwork across the desk as the office door burst open so hard it slammed into the wall.

Spinning around in my chair, I gaped at the man in the doorway. His dark hair and emerald green eyes certainly were something to notice. Why did my fingers turn white as they clutched the chair arms?

His face was livid as he thrust a piece of paper out in front of him. "If I get another complaint from Mrs. Sinclair about my TV being too loud after seven p.m., I swear I will take that yowling tabby cat of hers and pitch it right out the window! The only way she can hear my TV is if she's got a glass against the wall again!"

He didn't even wait for a response before tossing the paper at Sonya and storming out of the office. As soon as it felt safe to speak again, I asked, "Who on earth was that?"

Sonya sighed. "Baxter. Never mind him. He's always like that. Those two …" She shook her head again, but dismissed the whole encounter a moment later.

I wished I could have done the same.

"Anyway," Sonya continued, "if you have any questions about the lease agreement, just let me know. You'll actually be subletting from Bernadette since her lease isn't up yet, but all the same rules and requirements apply."

"Rules and requirements?" I asked. There were always rules, I supposed. Requirements? Like a credit check? I hoped that wouldn't be an issue as I had almost zero credit.

Tilting her head to one side, Sonya frowned. "Bernadette *did* explain how this building works, right?"

"It's an apartment building. How complicated could it be?" I mean, I'd never lived on my own before, but pay your rent on time, and don't annoy the neighbors. What else was there?

Slumping into her chair, Sonya's posture made it pretty clear there was definitely more. "Oh dear." She sighed and her smile was taken over by worry. "I really thought Bernadette would have explained everything already. I was so excited."

She said it like my staying was suddenly out of the question. Classes started the next day and I had nowhere else to go. All of my savings had gone toward tuition. I barely had enough left to pay the inexpensive rent for a month while I looked for a job.

"Why don't you just explain," I said warily.

Sonya bit her bottom lip, but nodded in a defeated sort of way. "My grandma, she's a little... odd." Sonya looked up at me, her brows knitted together. "My grandparents have owned this building forever, but after Grandpa passed and all the kids were gone, she was lonely and she made some changes to the standard lease agreement, but not the rent."

I was beginning to feel like I was sitting in the lobby of the Bates Motel, waiting on a key that would surely unlock my doom. "Changes? What kind of changes?"

"Well, there's kinda two parts." She took a deep breath, the kind a doctor might take before he tells a patient she has terminal cancer. "One of the reasons rent is so low here is because the residents all have a job... something they're responsible for so Grandma doesn't have to staff a maintenance guy."

"So, all the repairs are done by people who have no clue what they're doing?" I was suddenly wary of leaning too hard on anything or flipping on a light switch.

Sonya shook her head quickly. "No, no. Anything serious, we have a licensed repair person come in. Small things though, like changing light bulbs or repainting a scuffed railing, keeping the dumpster lids closed, things like that are the resident's responsibility. Everyone has a job."

"You're going to assign me a chore, then?" That didn't sound so bad.

"Well… Bernadette said you'd just take over hers."

Great. Just great! Bernadette the overachiever, who could do anything and everything, said I'd slip right in and fill her shoes like I'd never, ever been able to do before. I loved my sister, but we couldn't be more different if we tried. I had one talent, cooking, and honestly, I wasn't even sure I was good at that. It was just one of the few things I didn't suck at, so I figured I better attempt to make a career out of it since nothing else seemed all that promising.

"What was her assignment?" I held my breath, hoping for simple and easy.

Sonya eyebrows pinched together again. "Um, minor plumbing repairs."

"Plumbing?" I shrieked. Seriously? I had no clue where to even start. I was pretty sure I knew what a screwdriver was, but that was about as far as my mechanical knowledge extended. Daddy banned me from his tools after I tried to replace a bike pedal and ended up with my hair stuck in the spokes and one broken finger.

"You might be able to talk one of the other residents into trading with you." She tried to force a hopeful smile, but it died a short death. No one wanted to fish lost rings out of drain pipes or unclog a nasty sink. I didn't have to be a plumber to know that.

- 152 -

"So… the other part," Sonya said slowly. She waited for me to focus on her again, although zoning out in that moment would have been preferable. "My grandma really likes to be social, but she has a hard time leaving the building much anymore. Twice a week she hosts these, uh, dinners, and… you're required to attend at least one… per week."

It took me a moment to process that tidbit of weirdness. I had to repeat it a few times in my head to make sure I had it right. "Let me get this straight. Part of the lease agreement says that I have to hang out with your grandma and all the other residents at least once a week whether I want to or not?"

She nodded.

"What happens if I don't?"

"You get two warnings before you're given thirty days notice to move out." She looked up at me, her expression a mixture of hope and apology. "If that happens, Bernadette will lose her deposit and the option to renew her lease."

To me, that didn't sound all that bad. Sure, losing the deposit money would suck, but Bernadette had a good job and could easily afford higher rent to live in a building not owned by a kooky old lady who probably should have been living in a retirement facility instead of forcing unassuming strangers to be unwilling friends. Why on earth hadn't Bernadette warned me about all of this?

"The rules," Sonya continued, "are pretty basic. Rent's due on the first. Five percent late charge after the tenth. No loud TV or music after ten. No damaging the apartment. No physical violence against any of the other residents."

That last one slapped me out of my self-pity and shot me up ram-rod straight in my chair. "Physical violence? Is that a problem here?"

Sonya blanched. "Not recently."

I was going to die here. That was the real reason rent was so cheap. I'd finally moved here only to be roped into living in a funny farm where one of the other guests might kill you in your sleep for playing your TV too loud. Or maybe they'd just push you down the stairs. There were a lot of stairs here.

What had I gotten myself into?

No, what had Bernadette gotten me into? She was supposed to be looking out for me, not putting a target on my back.

I stared down at the final page of the lease agreement. One more signature to go. Clearly, Sonya was certain I'd walk away. If I'd had any other options—and I mean *any* other options—she'd have been right. Instead of running from the insanity of this place, I sighed and scrawled my name. As soon as I lifted my pen, Sonya grabbed both my hands and squealed in delight.

"I'm so glad you're staying. I was sure you'd walk away when I realized Bernadette hadn't prepared you."

Which is exactly why my traitorous sister didn't say a word.

Before I could come up with a solid plan to pay my sister back, Sonya was around the desk, yanking me up from my chair and out of the office. The clunk-clunk of my suitcase banging its way up the stairs sounded like a death march. I was so focused on my own misery, I didn't realize someone was coming up behind me until I was body-checked into the wall and another raised voice started ranting while waving a paper in Sonya's face.

"Is your grandmother serious about this?" a woman in her forties yelled. "She demands I come to these stupid potlucks, but now I can't bring my son? She really expects me to find a sitter just to show up to one of her weird dinner parties?"

A look of well-practiced patience settled over Sonya. "Marlene, you know Grandma is usually happy to have the entire family come to dinner, but Alonzo did take a magic marker to her walls. Anyone would be upset."

"He's just a little kid!"

As mad as I'd probably be about magic marker on my walls, toddlers weren't the easiest little beasts to control.

"Alonzo is ten, Marlene," Sonya said, which shut her up.

Ten? Seriously? Never mind. I would have banned the little brat, too.

"Why don't you check with Beth in room 330. She's the resident babysitter and I'm sure she'd be happy to help."

Marlene huffed, then spun around and marched away without another word.

Sonya shook her head and said, "Don't mind Marlene."

"She's always like that?" I finished. When Sonya nodded, I sighed. I was beginning to see a pattern.

A few minutes later, Sonya stopped in front of a door with shiny brass numbers of apartment 216. "This is you," she said. "Grandma's dinners are at six o'clock on Tuesdays and Thursdays, and she'll usually do something on holidays too. Everyone brings a little something and you only have to stay for an hour." She paused and bit her lip. "Really, it's not that bad. I'll be there."

She said that last part like it was supposed to erase everything else. All I could do was sigh in response. The only escape I was going to find was holing myself up in my new apartment. Reaching out with the key, I was jiggling it around in the lock when shouting from next door erupted and two doors burst open.

"I can hear your TV," an old woman shouted at an equally peeved Baxter.

"I don't even have my TV on."

The old woman spun around and stomped back into her apartment, slamming the door.

Baxter looked ready to do the same, but as he twisted around, he caught sight of me and glowered. "*You're* my new neighbor?"

I nodded, not daring to speak.

"Complain about noise once and …" His hands balled into fists as he tried and failed to contain his anger. "I don't play my TV too loud, no matter what that old bat says."

I just nodded again, hoping he'd go away. Granting my wish, he turned back toward his apartment and I released the breath I was holding.

"I got more than I bargained for, and I'm going to kill my sister," I muttered.

It was barely loud enough for Sonya to hear, but Baxter paused and looked back at me, his eyes narrowing before disappearing into his apartment. Feeling suddenly weak in the knees, I leaned against the wall to steady myself. That last rule about physical violence was looking more and more necessary by the minute. The best I could hope for at this point was that the residents were as diligent about not killing each other as they were about not missing dinner with Grandma Crazy Town.

***

BIO: DelSheree Gladden is a USA Today Bestselling YA and Romance Author. She lives in New Mexico with her family. When not writing, you can find DelSheree reading, painting or sewing.

http://delshereegladden.com/

Sweet Nothings

by Michelle McLoughney
Amazon Bestselling Author

She'd expected this. Maybe even wanted it. But she still felt a twinge of — pain, was it pain? No. More of a sinking ball of expectation in the pit of her stomach. Sitting alone at closing time in the restaurant, dressed in her favourite red silk dress, Kitty blew the fringe back out of her eyes. The stupid dress had cost her a month's wages, but her flatmate, Marie, had convinced her it was worth every penny.

It was a lie. A shield to hide the real Kitty Callaghan, who would have preferred to be at home curled up on a couch with her cat, Mimi, and a good book. There had to be a reason why she wasn't getting past first dates. If there was, it was a mystery to her, except they just never felt right. She blamed her addiction to romance novels. How on earth could anyone compete with such perfect men? Maybe she should read books about how to care for the forty-plus cats that waited for her to embrace spinsterhood. Kicking her shoes under the table, she drew a love heart with her finger on the tablecloth.

"Hey, gorgeous, why so serious?"

Kitty rolled her eyes, but smiled in spite of herself.

Matt had a movie line for every occasion. Somehow the quote from the Joker in *Batman* seemed fitting. Not waiting to be asked, Matt grabbed a chair and swung it around, nestling in beside her, his big body touching hers at the knees.

"Well sit right down and make yourself comfortable," Kitty said dryly, sipping her wine and twirling silky soft linguine around her fork. Bringing it to her lips, she sighed and closed her eyes, savouring the rich creamy sauce. Opening her eyes, she cocked her head to the side and raised a perfectly arched brow at Matt's silent assessment. "Don't give me that look, Matt Ellis. The food is good here. I'd rather eat alone than not at all, whether I've been stood up or not."

Matt produced a fork from his breast pocket and stole a few ribbons from her plate. "The food *is* good here, right? I hear the owner's a bit of a looker, too. Easy on the eye, so the ladies say," he said, grinning broadly at her.

Kitty watched his caramel eyes light up as soon as the food hit his palette. "He's an arrogant idiot, that's for sure," Kitty replied, nodding her head.

Matt opened his mouth and eyes wide in faux indignation. "Hey, I may be an arrogant idiot, but my staff and customers love me. Plus, you have nothing to complain about. You get mates rates. Here, I'll throw dessert in for free, because of your *troubles*.

Kitty laughed at the finger quotes and punched him lightly on the arm.

Matt sniggered and rubbed his bicep dramatically.

Kitty's eye followed the movement with interest. *Hey! When did Matt get so pumped?* Taking a sidelong peak at the muscles straining beneath his shirt, she felt her right eye twitch nervously. Matt was a tonic, plus being lifelong friends with a successful restaurateur had its perks.

"Soooo. This one makes… five?"

"Three, Matthew. Three dates in a year," Kitty said, clicking her tongue and holding three fingers in front of his face. She knew he was teasing and relished it. Bantering with Matt always cheered her up. She guessed that's what made him her best friend.

"Three potential husbands in a year and none of them made it on to a second date. Why is that, Kitty Cat?"

Kitty rolled her eyes. "Don't call me Kitty Cat. I'm nearly thirty. Maybe they didn't work out because they were all idiots who…" She stopped and tried to think of something to say.

Matt put a finger to her lips. "Who didn't deserve you," he finished, smiling.

Kitty looked into his eyes and returned the smile.

Matt cupped the back of her neck in his arm, his thumb caressing the softest part of her earlobe.

Kitty swallowed and felt her pulse quicken. *No! Not Matt. Not after all these years.* Whatever it was she saw in his eyes, she knew it was reflected in her own. He had been taking up far too much of her time. When had she stopped thinking of him as good old Matt? Matt, the friend. Matt, the go-to-guy. Pulling away from his touch, she frowned at him. "What're you doing?"

He pulled his hand away and opened his mouth, then closed it again with a snap. Jerking his head back, he stood up and knocked over her wine glass.

Kitty watched in confusion as he fumbled with a serviette and dabbed it roughly on the table.

"Sorry. Nuts. I've got to lock up. Wait for me."

Kitty felt her head nodding as though it belonged to someone else. He stood there for a moment, gazing at the top of her head, as though he had forgotten how to use his legs.

Under his breath, he said, "Tonight. It has to be tonight."

Kitty pretended not to hear, wondering if she had floated into an alternate universe. Matt was never nervous. Not Matt. He was always self-assured, always on top of his game. *Whoa, maybe he's ill! He looked fine. So… fine. Stop it!*

In one way or another, Matt had been the one constant in Kitty's life since she was four. She'd lost count of how many times he had rescued her or bailed her out of trouble. In some ways, she had depended on him more than a friend, even more than a brother.

When she'd wrecked her car in the snow two years ago, Matt was the one she had called. He had dropped everything and driven an hour to get her, a flask of hot chocolate and a blanket in the back seat waiting for her. The next morning she had opened her door to find Matt with the keys to a hired car dangling from his fingers. *Did I even thank him?*

When she had glandular fever from kissing Billy O'Brien behind the bike shed in primary school, Matt had shown up at her house every day and read to her. Even though she knew he hated every page of the soppy love stories she made him read, he'd never complained. Meanwhile, Billy O'Brien busied himself giving three other girls glandular fever. She had forgiven him, of course, much to Matt's dismay.

Whether as a pre-pubescent brace-faced ugly duckling or the swan she had slowly evolved into, Kitty had been diving headlong into catastrophes and Matt had been unapologetically bailing her out since forever. Up until now, she supposed, she'd viewed him as nothing more than a friend, a soul mate, a brother from another mother. Now something had changed. Something had shifted slightly between them. Kitty blushed when she thought of what lay beneath that shirt, how his eyes of liquid caramel melted her slowly into a puddle on the floor.

Stop it! Just stop it! I refuse to destroy a twenty-five year friendship over a silly crush.

Holding ice water to her forehead and cheeks, Kitty tried to calm herself. *Stop being an eejit for heaven's sake. This is Matt Ellis, your friend, Matt.*

Yeah. Matt, who at age fifteen, liked to stand beside her, fart and then walk off leaving Kitty red-faced and mortified. Matt who held her at her father's funeral, his arm protectively slung around her. Matt, who had punched Billy O'Brien in the face when he dumped her for another girl at the prom. Matt had dropped his own date off at her house before driving Kitty back to his place to feed her ice cream and marshmallows.

Who else has ever put themselves out for me?

Kitty watched him quietly as he locked the door after the last patrons left, and he finished chatting with the staff and the chef about the following day's workload. She loved watching him unnoticed. His face was a map of a land long discovered, with a silent language she'd been translating for years. Kitty recognised every nuance of his tone, every movement of his gait. She had been there at the birth of each faint line that creased the corners of his eyes… probably caused a few of them, too.

Matt turned toward her and walked up to her table where he stood silently watching her.

Kitty looked up at him and smiled. "What?" she said.

"You never got dessert. Wait here," Matt said, jogging off towards the kitchen.

"It's fine. Matt! Matt! It's fine, really."

"No. I have something special I want you to try. Just for you," he shouted back.

Kitty laughed, biting the side of her lip. Typical Matt who always came up with new ways to make her New Year's diet fail epically. After a couple of minutes, she couldn't stand the suspense and followed him into the kitchen.

Matt raised his head from under the long metal center Island and grinned widely at her. "Hey, you. Impatient as ever, I see. You never could wait for a surprise. Do you remember when you opened all your Christmas presents on Christmas Eve when you were nine?"

Kitty snorted and leaned against the stainless steel fridge, folding her arms.

"Yeah, Dad went ballistic and I ate Christmas dinner in my room," she said.

"Oh, poor Kitty Cat. You must have suffered terribly. How did you make it through your childhood in one piece?" Matt responded laughing.

Kitty grinned, watching as he piped fresh cream into some sort of chocolatey deliciousness in front of him. "Shut up, Matt! My Christmas was ruined. Then you gave me a mix tape, do you remember?" Kitty bumped herself off the fridge door and moved over beside him, grabbing a strawberry from a punnet and popping it into her mouth. Lifting herself up onto the Island beside him, she sat down on the cool metal surface and crossed her legs. His breath caressed her cheek as he bent his head to work, and she closed her eyes and inhaled the spicy scent of aftershave.

"Of course I remember. I gave you a mix tape every Christmas for ten years."

"Why did you stop?" Kitty asked, curious.

"Because you got an iPod. There just didn't seem any point anymore," he said, moving around her to get different ingredients.

Kitty frowned. *Did I give him the impression that I didn't care anymore? Should I tell him I kept every tape he ever made for me?*

"And voila! Okay, Kitty. Close your eyes."

"Why?" Kitty asked, before holding her hands up in submission when Matt put his hands on his hips in frustration. "Sorry Matt. Forget I asked. I trust you. Here, okay, okay. Closing them in 3... 2... 1," she said giggling.

"Both of them! Kitty Callaghan, you are impossible! Close both eyes."

Kitty grinned and shut her eyes, sensing his movement as he came closer.

"Open your mouth," Matt said.

Kitty wondered if his voice had always sounded so sensual to her ears. Like music that finds a place in your heart, makes a little home there and claims squatter's rights. Opening her mouth, Kitty waited until she felt his fingers against her lips and something soft landed on her tongue. Her mouth exploded with sweetness and she groaned aloud. "Oh, my goodness, Matt. What is it? It's divine."

"Taste it, Kitty. Tell me what you taste."

Kitty concentrated, licked her lips and smacked them together. "I taste choux pastry, chocolate, cream and caramel. Something else, too. Wait, sea salt. Salted caramel profiteroles?" She heard Matt's low laugh, and a slow clap.

"Well done, Madam. Indeed, it is sea salted caramel profiteroles. You approve?"

Kitty nodded quickly. "Do I ever. Can I open my eyes?"

"Not yet, young lady. Try this one. Open wide. This one is a torte."

Kitty lost herself in the indulgence of it all. Opening her mouth wide, she felt a spoon tap her bottom teeth as she pulled the torte into her mouth.

"This one, Matt. Oh wow. This one is orange chocolate. You really have outdone yourself. You need to feed me this every day for the rest of my life." She waited for Matt to comment and when nothing came she opened her eyes.

He had his back to her, one hand on the fridge door, the other in his hair. "Be mine, Kitty."

Kitty shook her head slowly and stared at his back. "Get wine? Is that what you said?"

"Be mine, Kitty," Matt repeated, turning around. "I said… be mine." He moved over to stand in front of her.

Sliding down onto her feet, Kitty took a small step forward, and leaned into his body, her arms around his waist, and her cheek resting on his warm throat.

He dropped his chin onto her hair and rubbed the top of her head in a gesture that spoke of love and affection. Their movements were in sync and natural, as though they'd stood like this so many times before. They had. This time it was different. This time it mattered so much more.

Kitty mumbled into the bare flesh deep in his throat. "If this is a joke, I swear I'll thump you."

Matt ran his hands through her long brown hair and tugged her head back gently. Dropping a kiss lightly on her forehead, he grunted. "It wouldn't be the first time you hit me, would it? You bullied me relentlessly."

"Matt!" Kitty squealed as he dug his fingers into her sides.

He held her tightly to his chest and wrapped both arms around her neck. "I've never been more serious, Kitty. It's always been you for me. Every year, I hoped you'd notice me, too. Every time you went on a date, I hoped he'd be an idiot. I wanted to be the one to take you out, to hold your hand in public, to hold your body next to mine."

"I don't want to lose our friendship," Kitty said gazing up at him.

Matt dropped his hands and stood back, shaking his head.

Kitty's heart clenched at the look of disappointment that flashed across his features.

Exasperated, he said, "Well, I should have known you wouldn't feel the same. You'd rather go for a jerk who'd hurt you rather than take a chance on love."

Kitty folded her arms and felt her hackles rise. If she *was* in fact a Kitty Cat, her fur would be standing straight up in defensive reproach.

"I beg your pardon, Matt Ellis! Don't take that tone with me. You are not my parent. I am my own boss. How many times have I told you that?"

Grinning and folding his arms in typical Matt fashion, he replied, "I've lost count. But I reckon it must be in the thousands by now."

Simultaneously snorting, tapping her foot and folding her arms, Kitty said, "Well, you obviously never listened."

Matt touched his finger to his lip, motioning towards her.

"What?"

"You have chocolate on your lip," he said.

Kitty brushed her hand over her mouth and licked her lips. "Gone?"

Matt laughed and shook his head. Rubbing his finger gently at the side of her mouth, he kept his eyes on her face and sucked his finger between his teeth.

Kitty stared at him, suddenly overcome with shyness. *What is happening to me?*

"All gone," Matt said. With that, he pushed her back against the Island and played with a long strand of hair between his thumb and forefinger. With a protracted sigh, he said, "You've been a part of my life since you were four, and I was six. I think I'm an authority on all things *Kitty* related. I know you, Kitty. I know your soul and your beautiful heart. I know you. I know you," he repeated.

Kitty felt as though she were coming apart at the seams. She was afraid. Afraid to let go. Afraid to love him and lose him. Afraid of a life without Kitty and Matt. Matt and Kitty.

"I want you, Kitty, and deep down, I think you want me, too. If you're brave enough to allow yourself to feel. I'm in love with you. I need you in my life. You already own my heart, so the least you can do is love it or let it go to someone else."

Kitty let the last scenario run through her mind. Matt with someone else... *her* Matt doing Matt things, but with someone other than her. It didn't bear thinking about. She gasped and heard the wobble in her voice as she said, "Don't say that Matt. Feelings aren't a joke."

Matt touched his forehead against hers and looked into her eyes. "Kitty, it's never been a joke. The way I feel about you is as unfunny as it gets. I want you, forever... not for a test drive. We've had that. We've had years of getting to know each other already."

Kitty put her palms flat on his chest and felt the warmth of him, his heartbeat strong and pounding. She swallowed, a lump like a ball of wool caught in her throat. "What are you saying, Matt?"

"I guess I still haven't said it, have I? I love you, Kitty Callaghan. I want you to be my wife. And lately I've been thinking that maybe you feel the same way, too."

Kitty dashed the tears from her eyes and nodded. "Yes. Yes, I do. I do. Whatever the question is, the answer is yes." She stood perfectly still as he lowered his head and pressed his lips to hers. He tasted like heaven, chocolate and the promise of something more. The promise of forever.

Later that night, Kitty unlocked her door and tip toed into her apartment. The light flicked on and her flatmate, Marie, stood looking at her, palms outstretched.

Smiling, Kitty pulled off her shoes, winced and rubbed her feet.

"Well?" Marie asked impatiently.

"Well what?" Kitty answered teasing.

"Did you have a good night?"

"Marie," Kitty replied, "I got more than I bargained for. Sit down, I've something to tell you."

*****

BIO: Michelle McLoughney is the author of the Amazon bestselling Saga, The O'Malleys. She lives in County Clare, Ireland, where most of her novels are set. Michelle began writing at a young age and won her first national poetry competition at seventeen.

http://www.michellemcloughney.com

Orphan Train

by Caroline Grace
Short Story Contest Winner 2013

Hannah perched erect on the edge of her seat, eyes scanning the sea of children, rapidly, rhythmically. "James, sit up straight. They'll be looking at you as we come into the station."

Child number 8 complied accordingly.

"Everyone, be sure your red number is attached and visible." Directing her attention to the sniffling child two rows ahead, she said, "Katie, come here. It's okay, sweetie… your brother has a new family now. When you get older, you can go visit him. Maybe it'll be your turn this time."

Hannah pulled child number 20 closer with her right arm, all the while sheltering another tiny warm body against her left side.

Two older boys squirmed in their seats, jostling the small children they held in their laps. It was time to wake their tiny charges.

"Next stop, Greenville. Ten minutes to Greenville," came the announcement from the conductor.

Hannah's eyes fluttered shut in prayer. She was grateful to have made it this far; grateful that each of these 21 little souls had survived the journey with her.

The spring rains had been particularly torrential, unpredictable, and deadly that year in the Midwest. The farm fields between Hamilton, OH, and Middletown swirled with muddy flood waters that threatened to overtake the train tracks beneath them, a precursor of terrors to come. Farther down the tracks, the train trestle near Middletown was completely submerged. The engineer, unable to back the train up or turn it around, did the only thing he could do--ease the train forward across the flooded trestle. The floods raged against the bridge and threatened to break it loose from its trusses as the train plunged deeper into the blackness that submerged its path.

Miraculously, most of the children slept when the attendant came through and whispered to Hannah, "God help us all, Ma'am." And somehow He did, for they made it safely across without being washed away in the muddy undertow.

Hannah wondered how the history books would remember the flood of 1913, but she was fairly certain they would be a good deal kinder in the retelling than they had been in the living. The little bundle resting against Hannah's left side stirred, yanking Hannah back to the present. "Iva Mae, sweetie, we're almost to Greenville. Please wake your brother and get ready."

"Oh, we don't need to go, Miss Hannah. Me and Elmer know nobody wants us. I'm too skinny and he's too little. Besides, if I got picked, who would take care of him?" Iva Mae put her arm around Elmer in a protective motion. Their older siblings had already been claimed by needy families at previous stops. They were strong and able-bodied, suited for farm work.

Hannah smiled. That little girl never failed to lighten her mood with her precocious comments and quick smile. It was, in fact, likely true that no one would choose Iva Mae and Elmer. It had happened at Fairfield, then at Hamilton, and again at Middletown.

The orphans paraded out onto the train platform to be examined, poked, and interrogated by the farmers and families of the community, most of whom were desperate for farm help.

Hannah tilted Iva Mae's chin up so that the girl's twinkling blue eyes were looking directly into her own. "Let's make a deal, okay? You and Elmer go out on the platform in Greenville. If no one takes you this time, you can stay inside at the next stop. Deal?"

Perfect lips parted into a perfect smile and a perfect heart-shaped face nodded under perfect golden ringlets. Half of Hannah's heart wished the strangers already gathered at the Greenville platform could afford to value beauty and innocence over work-worn hands and sun-beaten muscles. She knew the little girl would ultimately be happier with a family. Inwardly, though, part of her heart melted in relief each time Iva Mae re-boarded the train and snuggled up against her for the next leg of their journey.

It wasn't that Hannah didn't know the rules; she could recite them by heart: "The successful placement agent understands how to handle children. The successful placement agent avoids becoming emotionally attached to the orphans." Miss Acomb, the director of the Children's Home, repeated her mantra at every staff meeting, until all the agents quoted her proudly, wearing the recitation as a badge of accomplishment.

All the agents except Hannah. As one of the most senior agents, Hannah understood the reasons behind Miss Acomb's words, but those reasons came too late. Iva Mae Teeters had owned real estate in her heart since the first day she and her siblings arrived at the Children's Home.

Hannah had been on duty when the seven Teeters children approached the orphanage with their parents last October. She had motioned her fellow housemother to a back window. "Look at them, Dorothy. On foot, every one of them, and not passing a word between them."

"It's not nice to say, but they don't look very clean, and their clothes are raggedy. They surely aren't dressed warm enough for a day like today. Not a one of them has a wrap."

Hannah watched as the mother's hand flew up repeatedly to cover her mouth. "That poor soul," she said, pointing to the woman, "I don't think she's well. She has a terrible cough -- watch her." And then, "Oh my, Dorothy. That's the saddest thing I've seen in a while."

Both women fell silent as the children's father, a slim, hunch-shouldered man in shirt sleeves, turned his back while his wife kissed each child on the forehead. Without a word, the couple walked away, retracing their steps, not once looking back.

Still observing the children through the back window, Hannah spoke quietly. "Those poor babies."

The children watched until their parents were out of sight. When they could no longer be seen, the eldest opened the door and led his siblings inside. The boy motioned his siblings to sit on the floor while he approached the young man at the reception counter. "We're the Teeters, and our Ma and Pa cain't keep us no more. Our mama's sick and our farm got flooded." His voice cracked, but he struggled on with what surely was a rehearsed speech. "This here's the girls – Lillie, Flora, Elvina, and Iva Mae. Us boys is William, baby Elmer, and me. I'm Joseph." He dropped his head and quickly swiped his eyes. Apparently finished, he sat next to his shivering siblings and waited. When one of the younger children started to whimper, Joseph simply shook his head with a great amount of authority for one so young. The whimpering stopped, but the tears kept coming, and proved infectious. Within minutes, all six younger children streamed tears, eyes straight ahead, small hands grasping desperately onto larger ones.

Meanwhile, Hannah made her way through the orphanage toward the front lobby, and within minutes, emerged from a side door. Barely a moment later, and most unexpectedly, she sat on the floor with the children, gathered little ones into her arms, onto her lap, and close against each side, comforting, soothing, and stroking curly heads. In retrospect, she realized that in those first moments, she loved the little girl now looking into her face.

"Greenville, next stop. Now arriving Greenville."

Taking Iva Mae by the hand, who in turn held tight to Elmer, Hannah moved through the aisles, wiping smudges off little faces, cautioning restless imps to be on their best behavior, and reminding the older to watch over younger charges.

"Children, be sure your numbers are straight." Hannah's practiced hands gave a tug here and a pat there as she continued. "Now don't forget your suitcases -- they contain a new set of clothes and a coat for each of you. Ready? And, remember, if you're chosen, I will be around next spring to visit and make sure you're happy and well."

"Yes, Ma'am," came the unison reply, as at each of the stops.

Hannah had been at her job long enough to know that most placements would go well, but about 30% would be unsuccessful. The placed child may run away or the adoptive parents would prove unfit. She also knew such things resisted a remedy, so she dwelt, instead, on the 70% of successful placements. Some of her first placements were now married and had children of their own, and Hannah occasionally received a letter of thanks. On the darkest nights, she poured through her dresser drawer for such letters. This verse lay scrawled on a card in her drawer: *"Verily I say unto you, inasmuch as ye have done it unto one of the least of these my brethren, ye have done it to me."*

Every orphan train took a tiny piece of Hannah's heart, as she released the children to strangers. Unmarried, with no children of her own, the orphans became her family. As they entered Greenville, Hannah steeled herself for what would come next.

The screeching of brakes, the conductor's announcement, and the chatter of those waiting rang a familiar tune in Hannah's ears. Most of these folks had seen an article in the newspaper or an announcement posted in town about the orphan train. Some were there to choose a child, some were curious onlookers, and others just wanted to be a part of the excitement.

The train skidded to a stop, and Iva Mae skipped down the aisle toward the exit door with Elmer in tow.

Hannah motioned to them. "Stay in this little closet, and I'll be back for you after I get the line going outside."

"Yes, Ma'am," they said together.

She led the others onto the platform and lined them up for the townsfolk. As the last boy took his place, she held a hand up for silence. "Ladies and gentlemen, please form a single line. You may ask the children any questions you like, but please refrain from touching them. If you select a child, please bring him or her with you to the sign-out book at the end of the platform. Fill in all the information, especially the child's number so I can find you and the child next spring for visitation."

Her work at this stop nearly done, Hannah went back to retrieve Iva Mae and Elmer. Back on the platform, the three watched together as new unions formed. Iva Mae could hardly stand still in the midst of all the excitement, gawking and dispelling a dimpled smile on all who would receive it.

The first man in line, older and alone, passed up all the girls, but stopped to examine the older boys. "You... can you lift a bag of 'taters? Do you mind some hard work? You can have a room of your own, and a hot breakfast every day. Come on, boy. What's your name?" He stopped at the end of the platform to record his name and the boy's name, Charles Gibson. And #5 was gone.

The next couple stepped forward, and Hannah met their cold blue eyes. She tucked Iva Mae and Elmer in closer, relieved when the couple signed out one of the older boys. And #8 was gone. Scanning the crowd, Hannah was startled to find a man and his wife toward the back of the line studying her with open curiosity. For a moment, Hannah appreciated how her orphans must have felt. In self-defense, she stared back, and was again surprised when the man's face broke into a sunny smile. It was the kind of smile that lit up his whole face, the kind of smile that made Hannah smile back in spite of herself. She was amused as he poked his wife and pointed in her direction. Hannah thought the woman looked...well, "comfortable." Yes. Just plain comfortable. The comfortable woman waved and Hannah found herself waving back. Even from a distance, the woman somehow exuded a common sense and capability that impressed Hannah. Did she know these folks? She didn't think that was likely.

She looked back just in time to see one of the girls walk off the platform, hand in hand with a friendly-looking younger woman. Hannah smiled and waved goodbye, fervently hoping the best for the little girl. And #20 was gone. Hannah was still waving when she felt a tap on her shoulder, and looked over to see the comfortable woman and her husband had come up the back steps to speak to her.

"Miss, we don't know you," the comfortable woman began, "but we want this pretty little girl right here. She needs some fattening up and some good ole home cookin'. I hope you don't mind, but me and Oscar just fell in love with her and we were afraid somebody else would snatch her up if we waited through that big line."

Still smiling, Oscar nodded.

"This little girl?" Hannah said, but she knew. Iva Mae.

"Yes, that one, number 14. Hi darlin'! What's your name? Did you ever have your own room? We've got a great big farm and a pony named Jeepers waitin' for you at home. And I know it might feel a little funny, but I want you to call me Mama just as soon as you can. And this is your new Daddy." Again, the man smiled and lit up the platform. "Now we can't take the little boy--just you--but you're gonna love it at our house!"

Oscar finally got a word in. "Do you like poetry, little missy? You'll like the poems from James Whitcomb Riley. I'll pull you in the red wagon, and we'll teach you to ride Jeepers! We're gonna have so much fun! Have you ever heard 'Little Orphant Annie?'"

"No sir, I haven't, but it sounds nice."

In an odd counterpoint to Hannah's melancholy heart, she was pleased that Iva Mae remembered her manners.

"Miss Hannah? Will you take care of Elmer?" Iva Mae kissed her little brother, then pried his fingers apart from her own, as a smattering of tiny tears finally leaked out of the corners of her eyes. "I love you, Elmer, and I love you, Miss Hannah." A quick hug, and #14 was gone.

Hannah picked up Elmer, and they clung to one another. Hannah did her best to comfort him as she blinked back tears. The line of townspeople had come and gone, leaving eight lonely children to carry their suitcases back onto the train. They needed Hannah's love more than ever now. "Don't worry, darlings. We have another stop tomorrow, and I'm sure you will find a new family. Shhh...come sit with me. It's going to be okay."

Day led to evening. Evening led to nightfall. One by one, the children fell asleep. Drifting in and out of sleep, Hannah prayed, "Lord, I asked for a job, and I came away with love, fulfillment, and happiness. I got more than I bargained for, and I thank You. Please take care of all of the children, and especially watch over Iva Mae Teeters."

Epilogue: This fictional story is based on the true life experiences of the seven Teeters children and is dedicated to my husband's grandmother, Iva Mae Teeters Staight Durr, an orphan who grew into a beautiful, talented woman with the help of loving foster parents.

Iva Mae was chosen by a family in Greenville, OH, who loved her, treated her well, read James Whitcomb Riley to her, and pulled her in a red wagon. She was never officially adopted, though she took Oscar and Flora Staight's last name and entered school as Iva Mae Staight.

Elmer was not adopted off the orphan train, but later ran away from the orphanage. He found farm work for at least two different families who provided him food and shelter until he was grown.

Iva Mae grew into an outgoing and colorful woman who loved gardening, needlepoint, playing the organ, painting and ceramics. She was a member of a garden club, entering her arrangements in the Darke County fair. She married and had two children of her own, Jacque and Barbara.

Iva Mae's older sister, Elvina, eventually found and reunited all of the Teeters brothers and sisters with the help of Miss Ida Janet Acomb of the Children's Home in Cincinnati. Some of the written correspondence between Miss Acomb and Elvina still exists today, and is held by one of Iva Mae's children. We do not know if any of the Teeters children ever saw their birth parents again.

For more information about orphan trains, visit this site:

http://orphantraindepot.org/orphan-train-rider-stories/

Information from this site was used in the creation of this historical fiction piece.

***

Trouble in Deed

by Brian E. Staff
Short Story Contest Winner 2014

I was too scared of my Aunt Beth to love her, but I certainly loved her house. Aunt Beth was a lanky, gaunt woman with a deep, resonant voice and an intimidating stare. She had short hair which changed color with the seasons, wore baggy trousers and voluminous shirts most of the time, drank her gin neat, and smoked pungent French cigarettes through a long cigarette holder. She kept her cigarettes in a battered silver case that had strange symbols engraved on it.

A lot of people visited with her. Women. Really beautiful women, which got me to thinking. Beth and her friends and her house struck me as strange and mysterious, which made her all the more scandalous and fascinating. When I discovered that she was a spiritualist, locally renowned for the séances she held in her "boudoir," her allure deepened even further.

Beth lived in a rambling Victorian-style house in a rural area about 20 miles from San Jose, California, and we visited her often when I was growing up in the Bay Area. As a young child I loved to explore her home, which seemed to consist of so many small rooms, dark passages and unexpected staircases that I would invariably get lost, causing me to shout and sometimes cry for help. That didn't stop me doing exactly the same on the next visit.

Beth didn't care at all that I rambled through her house on my own, and when my parents tried to stop me, Beth would say, "Leave him alone. I have no secrets," which caused my parents to exchange frustrated and concerned looks that I couldn't explain at the time.

I didn't see much of Beth in my later teens, and lost touch with her altogether when I went to college on the East Coast. But when I graduated, married Emma - whom I had met in my otherwise lonely freshman year - and came back to take a job in Silicon Valley, I decided to pay her a visit. My wife and I so enjoyed seeing her that we visited regularly, first for the pleasure of her company – she was a formidable raconteur and always managed to entertain and shock us with unconventional views and salty language, and later to support her as she fought the cancer that raced through her body and killed her in six months.

Although we had become firm friends in her final years, it still surprised me when a man who introduced himself as Beth's solicitor called to say she had left her house to me. She hadn't given me any idea that she planned to do this, which was just like Beth. I broke down in tears when I got the news, which scared my wife because she'd never seen me cry.

I was very sorry to lose Aunt Beth, but having her house fall into our laps was a Godsend. Our neighbors at the apartment we were renting in Cupertino were a pair of young Goths who loved heavy metal music and played it at an ear-splitting decibel level until the early hours. The other neighbors were a very old couple who hated wearing their hearing aids, so they played their TV at full volume from dawn till dusk. For all but five or six hours a day, our ears were violently assailed by Iron Maiden, Judge Judy, Black Sabbath, Bill O'Reilly and their ilk. On the day we moved, when we drove up to our new home in its peaceful setting, the nearest neighbor a hundred yards away, it felt as if we had fled Bedlam and stumbled upon Shangri-La. As we sat looking at the house, unable to believe our luck, an elderly man with an ancient collie stopped and waved. I got out of the car.

"You Robert?"

"Yes," I said, "and who ..."

"Fred Goontz," he said, and spelt it out. "But don't matter how it's spelt, it's pronounced 'Goons', so don't worry about tryin' to make it sound different. I'm used to all the jokes. Beth used to call me Goonie but we got on real fine. You need to know anythin' about the house, just holler. I live over there." He pointed to a ranch-style home with a chaotic but beautiful garden. "You're gonna have some questions."

"Questions? What sort of questions?"

"Never mind about that now. Just get settled in. Call me whenever. Bye for now." As he and his dog, Spike, began to wander off, he stopped. "I guess you've heard that expression 'I got more than I bargained for,' haven't you?" he said.

"Yes, of course, but ..."

"Just holler," he said, chuckling, and walked on.

I shrugged at my wife and she laughed, but I wasn't amused. I don't like surprises.

We didn't have many possessions, so moving in took no time at all. Aunt Beth's furniture was old but tasteful and of very good quality. As Emma and I both liked retro, we didn't want to make many changes, so it wasn't as much moving in as moving around, rearranging the layout here and there. That evening we sank into a huge, cushy sofa in the sitting room – Beth's boudoir – with a bottle of wine.

"Peace," said Emma. "Perfect p ... What's that?" An echoing buzz had started up, then stopped. We sipped some wine. The buzz started again, then stopped again.

"Hmm, weird." I said. The buzz came and went a few times during the evening, but compared to the noise in the apartment we'd left, it was nothing. Less than nothing. That night we slept, undisturbed, with the windows wide open. Paradise.

The next morning, a Saturday, I was outside fixing the mailbox, which was in danger of falling over, as Mr. Goontz walked by, Spike hobbling a few yards behind.

"Gophers," he said, nodding at the leaning mailbox, "they tunnel everywhere. How ya settlin' in?"

"Wonderfully," I said. I was ebullient. It was amazing how great I felt after getting my first good night's sleep since we'd had an all-night power outage at our apartment. "Oh, by the way, there was a strange buzzing noise in our sitting room last night, I wonder if …"

"Rattlesnicks."

"I don't think so," I said. I know what rattlesnakes sound like. "It was an echoing sort of sound, more like a muffled bell."

"That's the coosticks."

"Coosticks? Oh, acoustics?"

"Yep, been like that forever. They're in the crawl space. Noise echoes around. Used to disturb Beth's meetings, you know, when she was in touch with the spirits. Hah! She made it part of her act. She'd stamp the floor to get the rattlers goin', and tell the folks it was the spirits trying to get through. Hah! I'm gonna miss ole Beth. She was a card."

"Do they ever get in the house?" I asked. I don't like snakes, particularly rattlesnakes, and Emma was petrified of them.

"No," he said.

"Oh, thank goodness, my wife …"

"Well, not often. And anyway, they keep the rats down. Well, strickly speakin', they keep the rats up."

"Sorry, I don't …"

"They keep the rats in the attic. You got plenny o' rats, but they know to keep to the attic. She tried to get rid of em, 'cos they kep' eatin' the lectric wiring, but they jus' keep comin' back. I can smell my breakfast cooking. I'll be seein' ya."

As he wandered off, I sniffed the air, and sure enough, I could smell bacon. I went indoors, and stomped around the boudoir, then got down on the floor and put my ear to the bare boards, but heard nothing. I looked up and saw Emma standing in the doorway.

"What on earth are you doing?" she asked.

"I was... er... checking the floorboards to make sure they're not damaged by um... termites or something."

"And you're listening to the termites munching the floorboards?"

"Well, I ..." But I was saved from digging a deeper hole for myself by a cacophonous drumming coming from the fireplace, and not with even the most outrageous *coosticks* could it be a *rattlesnick*.

Emma knelt down by the fireplace. "Where's it coming from? It must be something up the chimney."

I ran outside. Perched on the roof, furiously hammering away at the metal chimney pipe, was an acorn woodpecker. Emma had joined me and we were laughing, but after gophers, rattlesnakes, rats and woodpeckers, I needed a change of subject. "Do we have any bacon?" I said.

That evening we heard the buzzing again. I looked around the floor, expecting to see a 6-foot rattler heading for my ankles.

"I wonder what that is?" Emma said. "I saw you talking to Fred Goontz earlier. You should ask him about it."

"I did. He said it was the plumbing, air pockets in the pipes or something. It's been going on for years. Nothing to worry about." I hate lying, but sometimes it's better than the truth. Much, much better.

When we went to bed that night, I was drifting off to sleep when a breeze made the curtains billow into the room. It was warm and the breeze was welcome, until ...

"Yuck, what the heck?" Emma said before burying her face into the pillow.

I ran to the window and shut it. "Skunk," I said, knowing it wasn't.

"No it wasn't," Emma said into the pillow.

"I'll ask Goontz tomorrow." I tried to stop myself from gagging.

"Septic," was his succinct answer when I waylaid Fred the next morning.

"How do we ..."

"Fix it? You can't," he said. "Beth tried any number of times. Had all sorts of fellas out here doing all sorts of things costing her all sorts of money. Nothin' worked. You'll get used to it. In time."

"My wife is very sensitive to smells."

Fred found that very funny for some reason. "Beth used to be, too," he said, when he eventually stopped laughing. "In her séances I mean. If it blew in the windows when she was talking to spirits, she said it was just the smell of evil hobgoblins and whatnot trying to get some attention. Nothin' to worry about. She had 'em under control. She was a card and a half." Then he started laughing again.

I told Emma the smell was from a distant pig farm, and only came rarely, under atmospheric conditions which didn't occur very often.

That night when we'd gone to bed, I heard a rustling noise coming from the attic above us. Fortunately Emma was asleep, so I didn't need to feed her another lie to avoid mentioning rats, which she also loathed (I was planning to tell her it was the wind disturbing loose roof slates). But then I spent hours wondering if a hungry rattlesnake would ever manage to get into the attic somehow, by climbing up a drainpipe maybe, and the image of a heavyweight rattler plunging through the ceiling and landing on top of Emma kept me awake for most of the night.

Things were uneventful for a couple of days, but as we sat in the boudoir one evening watching TV, the house began to shake like crazy, and the rattling under the floor reached fever pitch. All the earthquake training that I'd received as a kid went clean out of my head, and Emma and I just sat on the sofa hugging each other as various objects crashed and smashed onto the floor. It soon stopped, but it was the severest quake I'd ever experienced, worse than the infamous Loma Prieta tremor. We cleaned up the mess and left the TV on, then tuned to a local channel, thinking the earthquake was bound to come up as a news flash. It wasn't even mentioned on the radio news when we woke up the next morning.

That evening as I drove by Fred's house, I saw him puttering around in his front garden, so I stopped to chat with him about the quake.

"What quake?" he asked.

"Last night, about 9 o'clock. It was strong. You must've felt it."

"Nope, not a dicky-bird, but your house would shake if a cow broke wind in Wisconsin!" he said, chuckling at his joke.

I didn't see anything funny in what he'd said. "What do you mean?" I said, somewhat tetchily.

"It's yer foundations. The house is on piers. Half of 'em have rotted away and the other half lean like drunked sailors."

I asked him why Beth hadn't had it fixed.

"Hah, do you think anyone would be willing to crawl under her house with all them rattlers down there? And anyway, she didn't care. She made it part of her act, when she was having a séance and the house started rocking 'n rolling she …"

"Okay, okay, I can guess the rest, thanks," I said.

I had a cousin who was an insurance agent, and he arranged insurance for me, although he'd had to 'pull a few strings' to do it because the house was considered high risk, which I'd assumed was just because of its age and state of repair, or rather disrepair. My cousin told me he'd offered to do the same for Beth, but she wasn't interested.

"Beth didn't care 'bout the future," Fred told me. "And anyway, she figured if the house fell down or burned down, she'd likely be in it, so she'd never get to collect nohow."

Over dinner, my wife told me she had met Mrs. Goontz walking Spike.

"I asked her about the quake and she said she hadn't felt it," she said.

"She's senile," I said. Lying was becoming second nature to me. They slipped off my tongue with no help from my brain. "I spoke to Fred earlier and he said the quake had nearly dumped him out of his armchair, and he said his wife was senile." It didn't sound right somehow, and the puzzled look on Emma's face confirmed it.

"All in the same sentence?" she asked.

"What?"

"Fred said, 'That was some earthquake and my wife is senile,' just like that?"

"No, of course not. It's just that he thought we ought to know, in case we found her wandering around looking lost or something."

"And since when does being senile stop you experiencing earthquakes?" Emma said.

I felt sweat break out simultaneously on my forehead, under my armpits, in the small of my back and on the palms of my hands. Maybe my lying skills weren't so good after all. I went to the refrigerator to get a beer, partly to create a diversion, but mainly because I really needed a drink. "No, of course it doesn't, but it makes you forget things. If you can forget who your husband is, you can certainly forget a quake."

"Does she forget who her husband is? How can she do that when he's right in front of her most of the time?"

"I don't know. I'm just giving an example. Do you want a beer?"

"I don't drink beer. You know that. Had you forgotten, or had you forgotten I'm your wife?"

I sensed a big row on the horizon, a 'he said, she said' of mythic proportions, but fortunately the phone rang. It was Emma's best friend, who could never talk for less than an hour.

I decided we needed a break, so I booked us into a luxury hotel/spa in Napa for a weekend getaway. It was great. We didn't tell anyone where we had gone so there were no interruptions, no rattling, no shaking, no scuffling, no foul smells, no manic woodpeckers. Just relaxation, good food, plenty of wine and, best of all, the only lying I did was on a massage table.

As we drove back and neared home, Beth suddenly gasped. "Oh my gosh, where's the house?"

"What?"

"The house. You can always see the roof above those trees. I can't see it. Where is it?" She was shouting, but she was right. We couldn't see the house. We pulled up at the mailbox, and stared at the charred remains of what two days ago had been our home.

"Oh my gosh," I said at last, flatly. "I don't believe it."

"I'm going to be sick," Emma said, and she was.

Two weeks later, I was at work when the investigator from the Fire Department called.

"Our official assessment is that the fire was caused by a rodent biting through an electrical cable which caused a short circuit," she said. "We can't be certain, given the extent of the damage, but that's our best estimate. Someone with the right knowledge could have set it, but no accelerant was detected, and we don't have reason to suspect anyone."

"I'm just glad it's settled," I said with a sigh.

"Well, I'm sorry this happened," she said, "but your insurance will get you a nice place somewhere else."

I tapped my pen against my leg. "It was a very old property and really, I got more than I bargained for," I said and hung up the phone.

When I first met the investigator, she'd asked me what my profession was. I handed her my business card, which describes me as a Product Marketing Manager. I didn't think it would be useful to mention my degree in Electrical Engineering. I'm sure Aunt Beth would understand.

***

Meltdown

by Gargi Mehra
Short Story Contest Winner 2014

Do you remember that girl who used her weekend trips to the city to get her washboard abs waxed? When she told me she did that, I glanced down at my belly. I pictured the parlor woman approaching my soft wobbling tummy wielding a wax strip in her hand, much in the manner of an axe-murderer stalking his prey. The mere thought gave me shivers. A series of welts might form on my stomach and I'd never recover from the experience. My ample tummy would look all wobbly, and what boy wants his girl to look like that?

But the truth is – all I ever wanted was a flat stomach. I wasn't scared of peeling the wax off, but I'm terrified the waxing lady might laugh at me in scorn. I needed a really flat stomach… one you could flip pancakes on, one in which the bellybutton resembled an actual circle and not a little basin that accumulated water and lint when I wasn't looking.

It's no secret that I tried weight loss by visiting that museum of fleshy backs and wobbling buttocks called 'the gym.' It's actually a torture chamber that inflicts mental as well as physical torture. Physical, because of all the hard work they make you do, and all the weights they make you lift. I imagine the Egyptians imposed similar tortuous methods on the slaves who built the pyramids.

The mental torture stems from the fact that I was forced to stare at all the beautifully sculpted bodies. Men flaunted their biceps and women their abs.

Why don't fat people come to the gym anymore? I can only surmise they must be daunted by all the perfect people running on the treadmills and working the elliptical machines. I don't blame them. As a woman inching towards 'overweight,' I feel almost gigantic in comparison to the waifs strutting around.

I finally signed up for surgery because I thought you'd like the results. Our fifteenth anniversary positively demanded that I achieve Scarlett Johansson's figure. And you must admit my plans and parties have always been successful.

Mother said I shouldn't have opted for it because it's too risky, but I didn't really care.

I knew I'd look pretty hot after this, especially in a strapless black gown to show off my collarbones and toned arms. I even tried on a gown with slits to show perfectly carved thighs and calves. I think the look works for me. I think I'll finally get that casting call for look-alikes for Scarlett.

When I woke up from the surgery, I blinked my eyes. I could see everything clearly. None of that grogginess that people talk about. I came to my senses and glanced around the room. I hadn't seen it before the operation because they hadn't made it ready, but it had a few things that I requested.

Pink wallpaper, check. Triptych of roses, check. The sofa bearing green stripes was maddeningly ugly, and the lights were designed like basins. The sunny yellow curtains grated on my sense of fashion.

The nurse entered an hour after surgery with a tape measure curled through her fingers. She instructed me to remove my clothes and stand in front of the mirror.

I unbuttoned the gown with shaking fingers and she shrugged it off my shoulders.

I stood facing the glass, and my knees almost gave away. My shape was as perfect as I had requested before surgery – a tiny waist, sculpted abs, a thigh gap and jutting collarbones. But that's not what took my breath away.

My nose was transformed from the squat frog it used to resemble into a piece of aquiline perfection. They had performed a rhinoplasty! My eyes looked bigger, my skin glowed, wrinkle-free, and even the little bald spot near the front of my scalp seemed to be covered by hair. Oh, so much beautiful luxurious hair! I got more than I bargained for! I dazzled more than any Scarlett that rocked the silver screen.

It served Mother right. She troubled me so much when I told her I wanted plastic surgery on our fifteenth anniversary. Mom's real problem was that Scarlett Johansson wasn't 'classy' enough for me. I should have given the doctor a picture of Hillary Clinton as my idol, and then Ma would have been happy. Look at me now. How glamorous and perfect.

The nurse applied the tape to each part of my body. I didn't take my eyes away from my reflection. She wrote up my vital stats on her clipboard. I didn't need to peek. I knew the figures were perfect.

I had looked forward to when I would step out looking just like Scarlett Johansson. With you on my arm, we would have looked great together, but that will never happen. It was a mistake to think we could ever get back together.

After this procedure, I am officially out of your league. I'm sure you can find someone who is more your type, or should I say more your 'body type.' We're done. Now I'll rush through the brambles and chase a brand new hero who really deserves me.

***

Secrets and Lies

by Susan J. Nickerson
Short Story Contest Winner 2014

I smoothed it, fluffed it, begged it to cooperate. Nothing. I gave it a push. A punch. Still nothing. *Fine, stupid pillow. Be that way.* I threw it on the floor, slid out of bed and tiptoed over to my dresser. Pulling the drawer open just enough to slide my hand in, I felt around for my thickest, most important pair of socks. This wasn't my first spy mission.

Careful not to wake my little sister, Steffie, I made my way over to the staircase. My well-trained, muffled feet allowed me to make it down to the third step without a creak from the old, worn-out wood.

The bickering that had awoken me wafted up from the kitchen with a bitter smell, like a shot of cheap whiskey gone sour.

Grammy and Mom were at it again.

"What is the matter with you?" Grammy's voice rose. "What would possess you to not pull over for the police?"

"I don't want to talk about it, Ma."

"You're lucky they didn't lock you up! You're lucky your father answered the phone because, I'm telling you right now, I would not have come to get you. I will never come and get you."

"Please leave, Ma. I'm tired. I need to go to bed."

"What you need is a good, swift kick! That's what you need. You have two young, impressionable girls upstairs. Is this the example you want to set?"

Grammy didn't really want an answer. Nor did she wait for one.

"Your husband walked out and left you because of your drinking! You think that would've knocked some sense into your head! If you get yourself killed, or worse, kill someone else, I'm not going to raise those girls!"

"It was an accident," Mom slurred. "I didn't drink much, I just forgot that I'd taken something to relax. I was sleepy and I missed the red light."

Slam! Someone smacked their hand against something. Maybe the kitchen table. Maybe Momma's face.

"I am sick of this, Sheila. You're turning out to be no better off than your lunatic sister!" Grammy hissed. "You better pull yourself together or you'll end up just like her." The front door slammed. Feet stomped down the porch steps. The car door squeaked before it heaved shut. Tires crunched over gravel. The silence left behind was cold and sharp.

Grammy was gone.

Momma had a sister?

I crawled back to bed, pulled the covers over my head and fell asleep to the sounds of Grammy's voice. *Lunatic sister. Lunatic sister. You're no better than your lunatic sister. Slap!*

I looked at my alarm clock — how did it get to be eleven? The sun shining through my window did little to lift the dread from the previous night. I couldn't think straight. If Mom had a sister, then Grammy had a daughter, and Steff and I had an aunt. A-U-N-T. A true blood relative that had been secretly stashed away. Secrets and lies. My mother's voice was set on shuffle mode in my head. *I thought it was important to have two or more children. I didn't want you girls growing up an only child like I did. Only child. Only child. Lies.*

I had to face her. I did not want to. I wondered if she knew I'd been listening. Wondered if that might cause her shame. I threw on an old, ragged sweatshirt and a faded pair of blue jeans. I left my spy socks on, even though it was nearing the end of June. I convinced myself I could do it. I wanted Mom to know that as my thirteenth birthday approached, I was a different person, a wiser, more mature Grace. I could now be trusted as a responsible, reliable, young adult. It was important that she understood how I would stick by her. No matter what.

A red-eyed Mom looked up from the morning newspaper. "Sleep good?" She asked half-heartedly, and turned the page.

I was stunned by her appearance. The bride of Frankenstein looked better. And although her hair was combed and she was dressed complete with her make-up, the bags under her eyes were enormous.

The opportunity to talk with her woman-to-*almost*-woman was right there in front of me. I was going to do it. I was going to tell her what I heard and offer my support and understanding. I took a deep breath before I took my first step into the bizarre world of adults.

"Mom, I—"

She cut me off. "Oh, Grace, you gotta read today's Peanuts."

Peanuts? The comic strip?

"I love it when Peppermint Patty calls Snoopy the 'funny-looking kid who plays shortstop,'" she smiled. "She calls him a kid!"

Oh, Mom. Don't do this. Don't sweep the dirt under the rug.

"I just love Snoopy," she said.

I stood firm. I didn't back down. I was going to tell her exactly what I thought of everything that was revealed last night. I threw my shoulder's back, took a deep breath and looked her straight in the eye. "Snoopy's my favorite, too," I answered.

She looked me straight in the eyes and said, "It's your lucky day, Grace. I went out this morning and bought you something," Momma said and lifted her newspaper, revealing the box from Carol Ann's Bakery.

"Cool," I said, and we were done. Just like that. A jelly doughnut had been offered. A deal had been made. See no evil. Hear no evil. Speak no evil.

Sitting cross-legged on the splintery floor of the attic, I rummaged through some dusty old cardboard boxes for what seemed like days. I stood up, stretched, and grabbed another box. It was heavier than it looked and I dropped it with a thump. Inside was Mom's high school yearbook and a few old record albums. The Rolling Stones. Pink Floyd. Neil Young. Under the last one lay a photo album.

That's it! That's what I need! I was sure to find it brimming with family pictures. Holidays, birthdays, snapshots of Mom's life before Daddy. If I could find the unfamiliar face of a girl, or a young woman, I would just ask Mom who she was.

It was a beautiful, burgundy-colored book. Thick pressed cardboard formed the front and back covers, held together with a gold, decorative cord. I ran my finger over the raised, embellished letters: PHOTOGRAPHS. With great anticipation, I opened the cover.

I quickly scanned the crowded first page and recognized almost every magazine cut-out. Jim Morrison. The Beatles. Janis Joplin. Written underneath the pictures were nicknames. Groovy. Delicious. Scrumptious.

Not one family photograph.

Disappointed, I reached up to shut off the light when a quick flash caught my eye. I looked over at the direction it came from, but there was only a broken rocking-chair, piled high with stuff. I decided to investigate and moved Mom's large, half-finished, paint-by-number out of the way. And there, behind the painting, behind the chair, under a pile of yellowed lampshades, was a storage trunk. The flash must have come from the brass lock.

My hand was shaking when I opened the lid. The strong scent of mothballs took my breath away. The first thing I saw was an old, scratchy army blanket, a multi-colored, granny-square type afghan that screamed the seventies. My heart continued to race, as if I'd expected to find a dead body. *You're just nervous,* I told myself. *Breathe.*

"Helloooo," Steff yelled from the bottom of the staircase, "... anybody home?"

"I'll be right down!" I responded, hoping my little sister would not smell my anxiety.

Without any more time to search the whole trunk, my strategy was to get in, get something, and get out. I picked up a corner of the blanket and peeked underneath. More bedding. I poked around. A quilt, some blankets, a bedspread. In a last ditch effort, I reached under the heavy weight and felt around for anything that might not be bedding. My fingers brushed against something hard. I grabbed hold and pulled it up. It was a briefcase. Locked. I darted back down the creaky stairs, briefcase clutched tight against my chest. Once back in the safety of my room, I shoved the briefcase under the mattress.

After dinner, and after the usual boring banter was exchanged, I nonchalantly made my way back upstairs to my room. With great anticipation, I slid the briefcase out, hopped up on my bed and sat there for a moment, holding the dark family secret on my lap. By the looks of it, I was going to need a tiny key. I wracked my brain trying to remember where I'd seen little keys. Button Box! Hall closet! I stashed the case and before I could take my next breath, I was there.

The boxes were lined up neatly on the top shelf so I dragged the step stool over, climbed up the two steps and decided to have a look. The Christmas candy tin Momma had filled with one-of-a-kind buttons was right there in the front, waiting for me to open it. *This is too easy,* I thought. I jumped off the step stool, box in hand, and quickly lost my balance. Buttons, buttons, everywhere.

Using my hand as a broom, I swept them

into a small pile then tossed them into the tin, rat-a-tat-tat. I scooped up the leftovers one by one and dropped them in the box. I took one last look to make sure I had them all and spotted what appeared to be a tiny silver button that had slid beneath Steffie's rusty roller skates.

I pulled it out only to find it was a diaper pin with half a dozen small keys on it. Small like the kind that would open a jewelry box. Or a trunk. Or a briefcase! I tried with all my might to stay calm as I put everything back into place before rushing back up the stairs to my room. I pulled the briefcase back out and tried the first key. Nothing. My hand was shaking as I tried the second, then the third. Click.

Did I really want to know this? I wiped my hands on my jeans, took a deep breath and flipped open the lid. No scary monster or diabolical demon jumped out and I breathed a sigh of relief. Just papers, no danger, nothing to hurt me. Old copies of The Salem Evening News. One, two, three of them. A plain, boring, manila envelope.

I needed to hurry but the pages seem impossible to turn, heavy with the weight of someone's memories, thick with the burden of someone's truth, sturdy against my cowardly resistance. I took the first one out and looked at the headlines.

Local Woman Held in Attempted Murder

Salem — A woman is being held at the Framingham State Women's Correctional Institution on charges of the attempted infanticide of her newborn daughter. This according to Salem Police Department's Office report.

Lizzie (Spencer) Dupree, 24, is charged with assault and battery with intent to kill, after she attempted to suffocate her four week old infant.

Police responded to an emotional phone call placed by family members who told authorities that she had been suffering from bouts of depression after giving birth just one month ago.

Mrs. Dupree will undergo a psychiatric evaluation at Danvers State Hospital, where she will most likely be held pending a trial date. No family members were available for further comment.

I picked up the next one.

New Details Emerge in Dupree Case

Salem — State and defense attorneys agreed to appoint Dr. Robert S. Cooke, a well-known Boston psychiatrist, to testify at a competency hearing for the 24-year-old Salem homemaker, Lizzie (Spencer) Dupree, who is charged with the suffocation of her infant daughter in an attempt to cause death.

A trial date has not yet been determined. The infant girl has been released to the custody of her aunt and is said to be in good health.

I folded the newspapers carefully and quietly, although I was the only one to hear them crinkle. I creased the pages with respect. Powerful words deserve to be acknowledged and appreciated, whatever news they bear. The next newspaper was opened and folded to the page of importance.

OBITUARIES

Elizabeth 'Lizzie' DUPREE, 24

SALEM — Elizabeth M. Dupree, 24, of 12 Birch Lane, Salem, died suddenly early Sunday morning at Danvers State Hospital. She was the loving wife of Frederick W. Dupree, a long time Salem resident.

I stopped reading. So many feelings vied for attention that it was hard to pick one and hold on to *just that one*. Reason told me to pack everything up. Just in the last hour I got more than I bargained for. More than I had ever imagined. But reason never won in my head, so, I slid the boring manila envelope out of the briefcase and unwrapped the string that kept the contents of the envelope secure. It felt light, not even as heavy as a teen magazine. It was impossible for something that lacked character to hold any bad news. I slid out the papers, hoping for a happy ending.

I couldn't grasp the meaning of the words before they blurred together. I thought maybe the information pertained to my father. We'd never heard any specific details about his side of the family. But as I read it, reread it, then read it again, the names, the words, and the true meaning began to sink in.

STATE OF MASSACHUSETTS - CERTIFICATE OF ADOPTION

The door to Steffie's bedroom was always left ajar, just enough to let the midnight monsters crawl out. I gave the door a gentle nudge, careful to be quiet. Steff could be a grumpy-head if you woke her up. In the dark it was hard to tell what she had in bed with her, but it was big. A pillow maybe, or a giant stuffed animal.

A weird orange light came from Bozo the nightlight and dimly lit their faces. It should've been a red glow, like the clown's nose, but Momma insisted on buying the cheapest light bulbs ever made. Ten to a pack from Woolworths. No matter how new the package was, they always burned dim.

My intake of breath was quick and loud but no one stirred. I stared at my mother, sound asleep, with her arms wrapped around her youngest daughter. Adopted daughter. Niece. Whatever. For the first time I noticed how much Steffie looked like Mom, her aunt. The slender slope of their noses, the thin, heart-shaped lips. Steffie was a mini-Momma. Why hadn't I seen this before?

It was a good thing I could find my way back to my room in the dark because a flood of tears blinded me. I curled up under the covers and started counting secrets and lies like other people counted sheep.

Mom was an only child. Lie #1 jumped over the fence.

***

Wings Under Water

by Tricia Seabolt
Short Story Contest Winner 2014

"Victoria. Victoria!" A breeze laced with sea brine and cotton candy rushed across the beach, carrying my name.

"I'm *speaking* to you." Mother said, her voice more insistent.

"Victoria Leigh Mansfield, if you do not peel your eyes away from that disgusting creature this instant, you will not be allowed to go to the beach for the rest of the week."

A wave crashed over the shore, and I finally turned to face my mother who was draped across her beach lounger, looking as beautiful as a mermaid. Her red hair shimmered in the blazing sun and her ruffled bikini barely covered the parts it was intended to.

My sister, Sylvia, played in the sand next to her. She was being her typical three-year old self, squishing the remains of a Popsicle between her fingers.

"He's not like us," Mother said with a hiss. Her hand shot out to grab my wrist. I gasped as she yanked me down into the sand. She leaned in close to my ear. "He's not even *human*. Remember that." Her words were heavy with the sugary, peach daiquiri she was sipping.

"But why is he …"

Mother brought one perfectly manicured finger over her glossed lips.

"Shhh! All I want is a relaxing day at the beach." She sighed. "Do all 13-year old girls have this many questions?"

"He looks hungry," I said, ignoring her question. I glanced at our picnic basket, still brimming with the remains from our lunch. "Can I give …"

Mother looked as though I had just asked her to go a whole day without make up.

"Are you crazy? Those *things* are like feral cats. If you feed them, you'll never get rid of them." She sighed again and smoothed her hair. "If he's hungry, that's his problem."

"Who's hungwey?" Sylvia looked up from the hole she was digging with her Popsicle stick.

"No one, sweetie," Mother waved her hand dismissively, then lowered her voice as Sylvia went back to her hole digging mission. "Your father and I have tried to shield you girls from… from… *things* like that. But sometimes there is no escaping the bottom feeders, so I called the police." She tapped the phone that rested on the arm of the lounger.

"The police? But why …"

"Not another word. Now take your sister to collect shells." She lay back and took a luxurious sip from her drink.

I knew the discussion was closed, so I took Sylvia's little hand, and we wondered to the shore line. Her sticky fingers curled into mine. "I'm gonna get the biggest shell ever," she said. Her blonde pigtails bounced as she skipped along. "*Come on* Bictoe-we-a!"

"I'm coming," I said, forcing myself not to look back at the figure that hunched in a patch of sea grass just beyond the beach. The water was deliciously warm as it lapped over our ankles. I curled my toes into the smooth, wet sand and looked up and down the beach as Sylvia plunked shells into her bucket.

People lounged in the sand, cocooned in the promise of the summer that lay ahead on their exclusive, members' only beach. People like my parents. Rich people.

"One shell, two shells, three shells," Sylvia sang.

Every fiber of my body twitched, begging me to turn. Unable to fight it any longer, I gave in. My heart ached the same way it did when I first laid eyes on him. *He was homeless, wasn't he?* Why else would his clothes have holes and his gaunt face be shadowy with dirt? His knees were drawn up against his chest and spaghetti thin arms were laced around them. His gaze was set somewhere behind me. I thought about how lonely he must feel, watching life swirl by. Did he receive a birthday present? I wondered if he had a middle name and when he last had a cheeseburger. I wanted to give him one.

Suddenly, the man sprung to his feet as though he had been jolted with electricity. He began running with his arms swinging, propelling him forward. His matted hair flew behind him like a tangled web. Behind him, a police car had pulled up.

I was frozen as I watched the man weave between tanned bodies and colorful umbrellas like a gazelle. I realized he was probably running from the police. Mother was right about him being a bottom feeder. He was not only homeless, he was a criminal.

By now, I could see his eyes. They were wide and a deep brown. A scream erupted from my throat when I realized he was running straight at me. Nothing made sense except grabbing my sister and escaping this maniac. How stupid I had been to feel sorry for him. My arms flailed blindly as I reached for my sister. A flash of yellow teeth glinted in the sun above me.

"No!" I yelped. "Sylvia!" She wasn't there. My mind raced as panic pierced my insides. I thought of her clear blue eyes watching me. Her voice floated through my mind, *"Bic-toe-we-a!"* Time seemed to stand still as the homeless man barreled toward me. There was no time to save my little sister. I squeezed my eyes shut and prepared for the impact that never came.

I opened one eye. Then the other. He had run right past me. Right into the ocean, clothes and all. It was as if I had been shaken awake from a deep sleep and plopped on a beach. The world slowly came back into focus. Colors and shapes sharpened, sounds flooded my ears. People were running toward the shoreline. Designer beach bags were abandoned and drinks were dropped into melting puddles in the sand.

"Sylvia! My baby. Oh, my baby!" Mother shoved her way through the crowd. Her beautiful features were twisted into an expression of horror as she sprinted across the sand.

What was going on? I turned so I was facing the vast expanse of ocean sloshing behind us. Icicles of terror stabbed my chest, and I struggled to take a breath when I saw what had grabbed everyone's attention. I dug my nails into my bare thighs and a scream froze in my throat.

The homeless man was tromping through knee deep water towards the shore. In his arms was Sylvia. Her usually perky pigtails hung limply, and her little pink body was pale and lifeless. Briny ocean water dripped off my precious sister. More than anything, I wanted her to leap from his arms to continue her search for the biggest shell ever.

What had I done? What had I done? I was supposed to be watching her. Instead, I had let my sister wander off. I had failed her.

The man stumbled onto the shore and deposited Sylvia into the wet sand.

"My baby. My baby!" Mother was hysterical as she collapsed onto the sand next to her little girl.

The policeman appeared, and we all watched as the man performed CPR.

A hot breeze rolled across the beach and endless, frothy waves bubbled over the shoreline. My sister's overturned bucket waited for her return.

Mother clawed at the sand, begging my sister to breathe.

Hot tears spilled down my cheeks and I prayed she would be alright. Then there was a little sputter, followed by an eruption of cheers from the crowd. I opened my eyes cautiously, slowly. My heart leapt when Sylvia's chubby little arms fluttered and she coughed. *If she was coughing, she was breathing!*

"Oh my darling I'm here. I'm here," soothed Mother.

I shoved my way through the crowd and crumpled in the sand next to her. Somewhere in the distance, there was a wail of sirens. After the red-faced policeman helped clear the water from her lungs, mother thanked him through mascara-colored tears.

"I'm so sorry, Sylvia. Big sis is so sorry," I whispered and planted kisses on her round cheeks, relishing the warmth of them.

She stared at me with those clear, trusting eyes. "It's okay, Bic-toe-we-a. Can I have a snow cone?"

The sound of her voice dipped into my insides to stir away the blackness that had been there only moments before.

"Oh, darling, you can have all the snow cones your heart desires," Mother said, scooping her up and cradling her like a baby. For once, she didn't care that Sylvia's sandy legs were leaving muddy streaks all over her.

Before I could tell Sylvia how much I loved her, a paramedic took her to check her over. He assured us that she would be fine and this was standard procedure.

Mother surprised me by wrapping me in a hug. "I love you," she whispered into my hair.

"I'm so sorry. This is all my fault …" I stopped mid-sentence.

Mother was not listening. Her eyes were scanning the crowd that swarmed around us. "Where is he?" she said.

"Your husband is working," one of Mother's busy body friends said.

"He is not my husband!" Mother said through clenched teeth. She leaped to her feet, shielding her eyes from the sun as she scanned the people.

"Well then, who are you looking for, dear?" Mrs. Johnson said, patting Mother's arm. "You've just been through quite a trauma... maybe you should sit."

"Don't tell me what to do," Mother said. "Where is he? Where is the man who saved my baby?"

The man. Not the thing.

"The police officer is right there, dear." Mrs. Johnson motioned to the officer who was in deep conversation with one of the paramedics.

"I'm talking about the man who pulled Sylvia out of the water. The one who laid her on the beach." Mother was pacing back and forth.

Mrs. Johnson chewed on her bottom lip. "Honey, Sylvia was *found* on the shore. There was no man. We *all* saw her there. A wave sucked her in and thank the dear Lord, brought her right back."

"The wave didn't bring her back," Mother insisted. "*He* brought her back. Victoria saw him. Just ask her."

Mrs. Johnson's furry eyebrows raised in my direction as she gave me a *your Mother is going crazy* look.

I came to Mother's rescue. "Of course I saw him. The homeless man with the tangled hair. He saved my sister's life."

Mrs. Johnson clucked her tongue and leaned into the officer who had performed CPR on Sylvia. "Officer, I think they may be going a little hysterical with the events of the morning."

"I am not hysterical," mother screamed. "Where is the man who pulled my baby out of the water?"

"Ma'am, your daughter was lying on the beach when I got to her."

"You're wrong," I cut in. "The man ran into the water and pulled her out."

Mrs. Johnson shot the officer a triumphant look, but he ignored her.

"I was called here with the report of a man loitering on the beach, so I got more than I bargained for. But I never encountered a homeless man."

Mother didn't seem to hear him as she buried her head in her hands. "I was so wrong about him," she moaned.

The officer scribbled something on his pad of paper and said, "Once everything settles down, you'll begin to see things more clearly. More importantly, you'll keep a closer eye on your children."

Mother was not used to being scolded by anyone, but instead of anger and defensiveness, Mother's eyes were round with tears. "I made a lot of mistakes today, officer," she said softly.

She reached out to squeeze my hand, because we would be forever grateful that the most unexpected set of eyes had been watching Sylvia that morning. Even though we would never know if he was an angel who walked this earth or one who had been sent here for a short visit, he changed our lives. Not only had he saved my sister's life, but he had taught us how to live our lives.

***

Weeping Willow

by Jamie Hathaway
Short Story Contest Finalist 2015

The first time I see him is at the willow. At first, I'm startled and then aggravated that someone is at my spot. But when he turns and smiles with one arm holding the lowest branch, I am struck. I'd wanted to be alone, to lie on my back, run my fingers through the dirt, longing to return to it, but now there is an intruder.

Intrusion. I decide to stay, hoping he will take a hint and go. But when I lie down, he lies right beside me. I shoot up with genuine surprise and I say, " What are you doing?"

"I lie down like this, too, when I need a different perspective. I just put my hands behind my head and look up. And sometimes I see things differently."

I'm so moved that I just look up. I was planning on looking down, but it does feel different. So we lie there, hands behind our heads, feet raking the soil from side to side, and we don't speak. Yet we communicate something to one another. And that is how we meet.

My therapist thinks it would be a good idea for me to journal, so I start with my moods. Mostly sad. No real reason to be. But I am. I had to take a break from school this semester, so now I spend my days walking or sleeping, going to group, avoiding my parents. They mean well but they really don't get me. I eat too much, then I don't eat at all. I am up most of the night, then all I want to do is sleep. I have ideas and then I cry at the thought of them. They are trying to understand this mixed state I am in. I am trying to understand this state I am in.

The second time I see him, we introduce ourselves.

"I'm Ry. I'm new in town. I've been here a few months. Moved from up north with my family."

"My name's Ruth. I'm 20 years old. I'm a student at East Carolina, or at least, I was. I live in town." I say this matter of factly, almost to convince myself as well as this strange new creature here at my tree. Instead of prying, he just moves on. He points at the initials carved in the tree. "I'd like to know the story behind these."

I hadn't noticed, but then at second glance, I could see the letters written by some lovers years ago. Maybe this was their spot back then. But it's mine now. And not his. He needs to go.

As if reading my thoughts he says, "You know this tree has more than one story to tell."

I just shoot him a glance. How dare he? He doesn't know me. But he kind of does. How does he do that anyway? I decide not to fight because it just requires more energy than I'm willing to expend at this point. I toss my yellow satchel which now doubles as my wellness pack onto the ground, pull out my favorite blanket and sit. I carry my favorites around to remind me to smile when I can't. It's my arsenal against doom and includes my lavender vanilla lotion, my pencils, sketchbook, and my camera.

Ry eyes my bag and says, "I guess that's not a picnic."

"No. I wanted to sketch the tree. There's something about it... so tragic, so beautiful, and sad at the same time."

He sits by me and answers, "Like you."

Like me. What does that mean? I guess I do look sad. That was on my chart. *Depressed affect*. But beautiful like the tree. Is this guy for real?

"I didn't mean it in a bad way. Just an observation," he says.

I decide to challenge him. "What's your story anyway? What did you tell me? There are other stories this tree has to tell, so, what's yours?"

He gave a small smile. "I come here to think. I left all my friends at home, and I just feel so alone sometimes, so I come here."

At ease for the first time around him, I say, "Well, that makes two of us then." And for the second time, we just look up and around, and I suppose our perspectives change a bit. Then I sit up to sketch the tree. I begin with the outline and then I remember. "What time is it? I'm supposed to see the doctor today in group. I don't want to miss it this time."

Ry says, "I never know what time it is."

I giggle. So much so that I shock myself, regain composure, and gather my materials. "I better be getting back. Next time I'll finish the sketch."

"I'll see you then. I'll be around tomorrow, same time."

I tell him okay and leave. What is happening is what I think. This guy doesn't seem earthly. Like a breeze from some far off place. He's not pushy. He's observant. He thinks I'm beautiful. He likes to lie on the ground like me. But I barely know him. Can this be what people mean when they mention kindred spirits? No. He's a guy. Maybe he's a little depressed too. Maybe he really does know how I feel.

Anyway, I go to group. The doctor increases my meds and hopes I will feel better the next time she sees me. So in group there is a new woman. Her name is Naomi. I was going to comment on the biblical account of our names, but when I learn that she was here because her son committed suicide, I decide against it. I think the correlation would be too painful. I mention my new friend but not his name or any particulars, just the idea of someone being interested in me, and I suppose me being interested in him, too. The group agrees that I don't need any relationship until I am better.

It's unanimous, except for Naomi. She remains silent with a pair of shades on most of the session. So much for group support.

The next day I meet Ry at our site. Our site. Are we an *us* now? We kind of are. I sketch the tree while he carves it, first his initials, then mine. Close but nothing between or after to indicate familiarity. I show him the sketch.

His knowing eyes stare into mine. Past my cornea into my innermost core... the place that frightens me so. And he sheds a single tear. And touches my face.

I place my hands on his, and our eyes never part. In those eyes, I see him... his intelligence. His compassion. His pain. And I want to know more. This moment is ours I think. Tableau. Eyes with knowledge. One tear. Now I understand the term I had trouble with in one of my lit classes last semester before I got sick.

He doesn't ruin the moment with words, but he does raise my head just enough to kiss my lips. The taste of genuine sweetness and sadness at the same time.

It reminds me of those lozenges from that story I used to read as a child. What was it? Yes. Because of Winn Dixie. His touch and taste are all I need to know... well, just to know anything. As we pull apart, I smile. The first smile in a long time. I got more than I bargained for. "I'm going to be okay." I must have said it out loud before I could realize it.

Ry just looks back in agreement.

I continue to sketch the tree and a thought occurs to me. "Do you think this is what Eden felt like?"

Ry waits to speak, pensive. "A place with no guilt or shame or fear. Yes, I suppose I feel that here. But if this willow did bear fruit, I can't say that I wouldn't be too curious to try it. We know so much as humans and yet so little still."

I just nod. His mind is like unexplored territory and I've only stepped in the general direction. I don't want to leave him or this moment, but reality will soon sink in. I want to skip group today and stay with him.

But Ry was reading my thoughts again. "You need to go."

"But I don't want to."

He just grins and leans in. "I'll be with you." And he kisses me again. He watches me collect my satchel and says, "Share this today. It's really good."

I tell him I will as I pick up the sketch of the willow. I turn to see him walking away in the distance. An afternoon sun beating down. Our tree centered on the meadow.

At group, when it's time to share, I bring out my drawing. I pass it around. Everyone comments on how much they like it.

Then it reaches Naomi. She puts a hand to her mouth and gasps. She looks at me and then the picture and then drops it to the floor before running out of the room.

I look at our therapist while picking up my book and say, "I don't understand."

She looks at my drawing and says, "Naomi's son hung himself from that tree. He was in terrible pain and had no relief. His name was Ryan and his initials are on your tree.

Then the book falls again. But this time, it is *my* gasp released into the air.

***

Self-Help

by Kathie Muir
Short Story Contest Finalist 2015

"I got more than I bargained for." Amy shook her head and glanced up at the psychiatrist. "It started so small... just a modest project that got out of control."

"That doesn't sound so horrible. What happened?" Dr. Jones paused to write a few words.

"I wanted a hobby. I watched a genealogy program and decided that would be my project."

"There's nothing wrong with that. A lot of people trace their family histories."

Amy grimaced. "I went a little overboard. I didn't think it through and jumped in feet first and head last. My goal was to write up the family tree in calligraphy for the entire family, showing our origins. It was going to be my Christmas present to them, although I also had an ulterior motive. I knew it would be less expensive than buying individual presents."

"Very clever... not to mention ambitious."

"Especially since I didn't get this idea until November."

"Go on."

"I went to the library for some ideas to charge my brain. Then I went on the internet. I figured I needed to learn organization first, so I emptied the kitchen cabinets onto the table, so I revolved my life around *it* rather than the other way around."

"I can see how that might help. Where did you eat?" the doctor said.

"In my bedroom. At first, I sat on the bed, but as the project grew, I sat on the floor and slept in a sleeping bag. I developed a little anxiety because towers of books were all around me. And then, because the kitchen was a total disaster, I couldn't do the dishes, so I ate off paper plates. One of my friends, or should I say former friend, was actually afraid she would get a disease in my house."

Dr. Jones scratched his head. "We're getting off-track, so let's back up. How were you doing on the family tree project at that point?"

"Well, that's going to be an Easter present now. I had to interrupt it because I kept losing things. Pretty soon I couldn't find my clothes, or even the washer. Between the stacks of books and notes, I only had a small path throughout the house. I found the TV though, so I took time out to watch '*Hoarders*,' thinking maybe I could get control of my life."

"How did that work for you?"

"It didn't. I watched the show religiously and took notes on how to change my life."

"That sounds promising."

Amy sighed. "Not really. I took so many notes that my one little path got skinnier."

"I can see why you would be anxious. I'm overwhelmed just listening to you."

"You have no idea. I just wanted to find information on my family and now I'm a major hoarder!"

"You have to stay focused on your goal."

"I would, if I had only one. I thought if I finished the family tree first, I could get rid of the books and papers and notes, but then if I did that, I'd probably replace them with calligraphy ink and pens, so what was the point? On the other hand, if I could manage my hoarding, I could organize my house and have room for the family tree."

"It's better to pick one goal and pursue it. It seems that you overthink things." The doctor said as he tapped on the desk. He glanced at the clock. "What happened next?"

"Well, I... but... I tried to ..."

The pen kept tapping.

"That is, there was a third option."

The pen tapped faster now, as did his right foot.

"What was I saying?"

"You said there was a third option."

"Oh, yes. So I decided to go to a self-help group. Birds of a feather and all that."

The pen tapped louder and louder.

"Well, if nothing else, I wouldn't feel so alone."

"And how did that go?"

"I expected to see a bunch of bag ladies pushing shopping carts full of miscellaneous trash."

"That's quite a stereotype," the doctor said, yawning. "Excuse me. Go on."

"And it was completely untrue. They looked like me. Apparently hoarders are able to compartmentalize their problems. You can look nice and still hoard." Amy's eyes teared.

"Why are you upset?" the doctor said, now with a feverish tap.

"Because I was the worst hoarder in the group. They said they'd never seen someone go from a normal life to a ceiling-high junky so fast."

"Did they give you any help at all?" Dr. Jones glanced at the wall clock as he kept tapping.

Amy sobbed. "No. When I told my st… story, they all felt so much b… b… better that they made me their mascot. Then they voted to disband. The decision was unanimous."

"Well, it wasn't quite that bad. There had to be one opposing vote, and it's good to feel that affirmation," the doctor said as he checked the clock again.

"No, it was unanimous. I was so depressed that I voted *yay* instead of *n… nay.*"

The good doctor rolled his eyes and tapped louder.

"At least you helped them."

"Yes, but then I felt worse about myself. I liked the idea of a group, based on the fifteen minutes I experienced, so I joined an OCD group to help me get over the trauma of the hoarder's group. After all, my hoarding could definitely be called compulsive."

"Yes, it certainly was, I mean *is*. Brilliant thinking." Tap tap tap tap.

"Well, it didn't work out that way. It turns out I should have been more compulsive about researching the group."

"Why is that?"

"They were all hand-washes and germophobics. Not only couldn't they understand my problem, they were absolutely horrified by it. Those crazy people spend their lives cleaning and re-cleaning where they've already cleaned."

Tap tap tap tap tap tap tap.

"I mean, every aspect of their idiotic lives was organized to the hilt. One woman slathered herself with sanitizer every time she looked in my direction."

Dr. Jones turned his head when the corners of his mouth turned up. "So what happened to the family tree?" Tap tap tap tap tap tap tap… much faster now. He checked the clock. Had the minute hand budged?

"Oh, yes. The fam …"

TAP TAP TAP TAP TAP TAP tataTAP, tataTAP.

"Where was I?"

"You were talking about the woman who used sanitizer every time she looked at you and then I asked about the family tree."

"Oh, yes. Sorry. Now it's looking more like… like …"

TataTAP tataTAP tataTAP tataTAP tataTAP.

"Like a… a… Memorial Day project. After being kicked out of two support groups, I had difficulty with motivation so I decided to join a self-esteem support group."

Dr. Jones took a long stare at the second hand on the clock. Was it working? He yawned. "You may have needed that, but perhaps it was also an avoidance mechanism. Go on."

Rata-tap-tap. Rata-tap-tap. Rata-tap-tap. The doctor ran slender fingers through his hair, giving it a slight tug.

Rata-tap-tap. Rata-tap-tap. Rata-tap-tap. Rata-tap-tap.

"That group didn't l... leave me t... time to ..."

Pen taps went off like a sub-machine gun bouncing off the mahogany desk.

Amy broke into a sweat. "Didn't l... leave m... would you mind not tapping that pen?"

Dr. Jones dropped it. "Oh, sorry. Where were we?"

"Talking about the avoidance mechanism."

"Oh, right. Go on." He tapped his right foot and rubbed his eyes.

"I was saying the class kept us busy. We had homework, including reading books. And assignments, such as going to a mall and finding examples of good and bad self-esteem in peoples' conversations."

"You were eavesdropping?"

"Well, yes. Kind of. The group leader seemed more like a frustrated camp counselor. I felt like telling her she needed her own support group for control freaks."

Dr. Jones glanced at his watch and smiled for the first time. "I see. Well, unfortunately, our time is up. We'll have to continue next time."

"Just one more thing," Amy said. "So I… I… oh dear. What was I going to say? I …"

"I really must go. I have an urgent meeting." The doctor held the door open.

"Well, okay. I can't wait for our next session."

"Yes. Me, too," the doctor said.

Dr. Jones closed the office. The paperwork would wait. Dictation would wait. There was nothing that wouldn't wait. A migraine loomed on yonder horizon. The first one in five years. Where were the Tylenols?

He headed for his car.

Thankful to arrive at his destination at last, the tension settled in his shoulders as he joined a room full of friendly faces. The meeting was just starting.

The speaker took the podium and wrapped the gavel. A hush fell over the room. "Welcome to the support group for psychiatrists whose patients drive them up the wall."

***

Winterkill

by Sharon King-Booker
Short Story Contest Finalist 2015

Winters in the Dakotas can kill. The wind
sweeps down, picks up snow, drives it in a swirling
mass, and screams like a tormented soul. Snow
drives against windows, trying to claw its way into
the warmth. When the wind dies, what is left is a
world of snow. Snow to make giant snowmen in
every yard but mine. My children always wondered
why I turned into a tyrant each winter. Now the
grandchildren just think their Grandpa is a little bit
daffy about snowmen.

In 1946, I was thirteen. The war was over,
and our farming community had fared well. There
were two gold stars still displayed, but those of us
too young to join the army were secretly sad that the
war had ended.

Our school building held all twelve grades.
All the stores and businesses were found along a
five-block Main Street and all were in need of paint.
Everything was coated with soot from the coal-
powered trains that came through daily. The houses
were mostly clapboard with wide front porches
where the old folks sat on summer evenings.

I was in the seventh grade the year that I got
more than I bargained for. The Murrays moved into
a house on the hill across from the cemetery and

they had three kids. Kenny had copper hair, wide gray eyes and freckles. Kevin's hair was redder. He was eleven and wore a mischievous smile. Kelly's auburn hair set off beautiful green eyes that kept changing and taking on new light and depth. Her pixie face made me think of elves or leprechauns.

Both my brothers were grown when I came along, so the Murrays became my second family. Their parents were younger than mine and they loved kids, so I spent a lot of time there.

They had the best Halloween parties. There were screaming witches, rattling chains, creaking doors and howls from their wire recorder. A huge, grinning jack-o-lantern sat on the porch, and a black cat with arched back and gaping mouth, menaced us from the living room window. It looked so real we had to satisfy ourselves it was only a replica.

Mrs. Murray heated cider in a huge cauldron. We bobbed for apples, played games, and made ourselves sick with overeating.

Later Mr. Murray scared us with the story of the Headless Horseman.

Winter held off longer than usual, but by mid-December, we had our first really big snow. I got up early that Saturday morning and went to the Murrays. We were going to have the biggest snowman in town.

With four of us working, he was huge. He had an old felt hat cocked on his head, an old green scarf wrapped around his neck, and a broken Christmas angel ornament in his hands. Strung holly berries made a belt, and a carrot for his nose. His eyes were made of coal, as was his mouth, and curled up in more of a leer than a smile.

Five-year-old Marilyn Beck disappeared the Tuesday night after the snowman had been erected. I was getting ready for school when Mr. Kaylee, one of our two policemen, called Dad to help look for her. I heard Dad say that Mrs. Beck raised the alarm when she didn't find Marilyn in her room.

The next morning, all the kids were talking about it. Jerome Hill, a classmate, said he heard his dad say there had been a big puddle of water leading from the Beck's front door to Marilyn's room, but no one believed him.

Sadly, Marilyn was found lying in the children's part of the cemetery, frozen to death. Clutched in her hand was the broken angel from the snowman. People speculated she had walked in her sleep. Fascinated by the snowman, she had made her way to it, taken the angel, and then awakened, lost and confused. The cold had done the rest.

After Christmas, we all trooped back to school. Nothing else happened until mid-January when Ben Scott vanished. Ben's dad was in prison and his mother took in washing for a living. Ben didn't attend school. We called him "dumb."

Kenny Murray, Chris Barrett and I had gone to the park to skate on the frozen Knife River and we found Ben Scott down by the bridge, babbling about playing with a snowman. He had a string of holly berries in his hands. He was still alive, although some said it might have been better if he hadn't been. He suffered severe frost bite and eventually lost both feet.

I started to work in Dad's store after school and saw our neighbors, the Murrays, only occasionally. There was something wrong with Kelly. Her pixie face was pale and pinched, and her eyes had a scared, haunted look. I was smitten the first time I looked at her.

This was a small town and everyone began looking at each other, sizing us up, so to speak. Both Mr. Kaylee and Mr. Russell, his deputy, walked the streets more often.

Red's Cafe was nearly empty when I'd walk past.

Mr. Hopper and Mr. Klein no longer spent their mornings in Dad's store.

Mom kept the doors locked, even in the daytime, and neighbors didn't speak much to each other anymore.

Mr. Murray was at the top of everyone's suspect list. He was new in town, and the family always had bunches of kids in and out of their house. Besides, the things found on the missing children came from the Murrays' snowman.

Several nights later, sometime after midnight, our phone rang. Dad answered sleepily. Afterward, he woke Mom and me. Kenny Murray was having bad stomach pain, and since the nearest hospital was twenty miles away, the Murrays were bringing Kevin and Kelly over for the rest of the night and wanted Mom and Dad to go with them.

When they arrived, I was shocked.

Kelly was pale and thin, her ever-changing

green eyes were sad. She was quiet and listless.

Mom made her a bed on the couch and sent Kevin and me to my room.

I waited until Kevin went to sleep and then crept out of bed and went into the living room. The full moon made everything bright as day. I could see Kelly lying on the couch, eyes wide open. "What's wrong, Kelly?" I whispered, "You don't look well." I sat on the sofa, stroking her hair.

"I can't tell you," she whispered, shivering. "You wouldn't believe me." She sat up, wrapping the quilt tighter around her shoulders.

I pulled her against me. "You can tell me. If I don't believe you, I'll tell you so." I think I knew then I loved her. She was so small, so delicate, so scared.

"Okay, but you have to promise not to tell anyone else. They'll think I'm crazy. The night Marilyn disappeared, I got a drink of water and looked out my window and ..." She shivered with the memory. "The snowman was gone!"

I looked deep into her eyes, wide and staring, but I met her gaze honestly and without blinking. "There," she said, her tone sad and reproachful, "I told you, you wouldn't believe me."

"I do believe you."

"I was going to show Mom and Dad, but I was so scared, I just went back to bed. The next morning it was back where it belonged and only the angel was gone."

"Did you tell anyone then?"

"No one would have believed me."

"What next? There's got to be more."

She nodded. "Yes," she whispered, "the night Ben disappeared. It was almost morning. I went to the window, and the snowman was gone again. This time I was going to call Mom for sure. Then I looked down the road." She shuddered and began to cry quietly. "It was coming back, its eyes flamed like little fires, and it sparkled all over, like it was covered with diamonds. It marched right back into its place and stood there, but the berry belt was gone."

I helped her lie back on the sofa and pulled the covers up under her chin.

"There's more," she whispered. "It saw me. It knows I'll tell. And it knows I watch it every night, all night. That's why I'm so tired."

"Don't worry, Kelly. I'm going to take care of your snowman."

"What are you going to do?"

"I'm going to see for myself." I still didn't believe her, but if that snowman was causing Kelly distress, I would take matches and wood and melt the thing. This was my chance to show her how much I cared for her. I dressed and crept from the house, gathered some wood from the woodpile beside the house, and, once out the gate, I ran down the alley two blocks to Main Street. If anyone saw me out this late, I'd be in trouble.

As I ran, the cold air seared through my lungs. When I reached the top of the hill where I could see the Murray yard, my heart leaped into my throat, then dropped painfully back into my chest.

There was only a patch of bare earth. The dark circle looked like a large stain of blood on a white sheet. I didn't know where to look next. I wondered if I should wait here or hunt for it. I remembered Kelly's description of its eyes, and that it knew she had seen it. Suddenly I knew where it was.

"Kelly!" I screamed. I raced for home, not caring about the stab of pain in my ribs or the sweat running down my face, freezing on the scarf wrapped around my neck. I could only think of Kelly. As I neared my house, I slowed to a brisk walk, entered, and removed my scarf, gloves, hat, and boots, and crept into the living room. I stepped into a puddle of icy water in my sock feet. Next to the couch was the snowman's hat, a shriveled carrot, and several lumps of coal.

"Kelly?"

She lay on the couch in the same position I had left her. The moon cast an eerie light over her face.

"Kelly? Are you okay?"

Her face was ashen, and wore an expression of pure terror. Her eyes wide and unblinking. She was dead.

I spent the next week in bed, not even able to attend Kelly's funeral. The doctor said influenza, but later on, I knew it was shock. I never told anyone what Kelly told me, nor what I had seen at the Murray home or in my own home when I returned.

The Murrays moved away shortly after. If they noticed the bare patch of ground in their yard, they never said so. They were too grief stricken following Kelly's funeral.

I hadn't really believed Kelly's story, but I wanted to support her. I knew I could never repeat it. Even with the snowman gone from the yard, adults simply didn't believe kids. The coroner said a high fever had caused Kelly to have a convulsion and that, in turn, had caused her death. She had, after all, been in failing health recently.

Now, more than fifty years later, I patrol the streets when the snow is on the ground. Faces peer from windows when they hear the crunch of my boots and they throw up a hand to say hi. I wave back and smile, but I'm really thinking of Kelly. I just keep walking and keeping an eye on all the snowmen.

***

Senior Class Prank

by Victoria Franzese
Short Story Contest Finalist 2015

When we were sophomores, we took the creative writing class that Mrs. Zimbalist taught each spring. Every Monday, she'd begin the class by reading a short story or poem that set the theme for the week. Using that example as a starting point for our own work, we'd create a draft and then revise and refine it every day until the end of class on Thursday, when we had to hand it in. Most of us put some effort into the initial writing process, but spent the rest of the week passing notes to each other.

Mrs. Zimbalist was a fairly lenient grader and she didn't deserve what we did to her later. After the first few assignments, we knew we didn't have to do too much to earn an A. She would circle the room, ready to consult with anyone who wanted advice on character development or word choice, but we soon learned that if we crouched over our notebooks and softly murmured something like, "I'm sorry, I'm not comfortable sharing this yet," Mrs. Zimbalist would move on.

One Monday, Mrs. Zimbalist read us the poem, *Mirror,* by Sylvia Plath. She said she had pioneered a kind of confessional poetry, writing about real events from her own life, including sex, relationships and motherhood in an open and unvarnished way.

That week, Cindi Brawner submitted the lyrics for the Journey song, *Open Arms*, as her own confessional poem. She had become obsessed with the song ever since Steve, whom she believed to be the love of her life, had sung it to her with great passion in the back of his van. Cindi had insisted that Mrs. Zimbalist would recognize the words, as the song was constantly on the radio. "She's like, a thousand years old," Cindi said, referring to Mrs. Zimbalist. She doesn't know a thing about music. Trust me, she'll never know."

Even those of us who had agreed with Cindi weren't surprised when she was summoned for a private consultation at the beginning of Friday's class. We assumed she would get in big trouble for plagiarism. Most of us were betting she'd get more than just a detention or two. Instead, Mrs. Zimbalist gently talked to her about being in love and expressing that love in the right way.

Cindi was visibly shaken by the whole thing. "It was the kind of conversation I'd expect to have with my mother, if Mom weren't so afraid to talk about anything that matters. I mean, she barely said anything when I had my first monthly, and I had no clue what was going on."

I remembered her telling me how annoyed her mom had been when Cindi asked questions.

She had a wistful look on her face as she continued, "Come to think of it, I kinda wish Mrs.

Zimbalist had been around for that."

A year later, we had Mrs. Zimbalist for our junior class in American Literature. Although she was happy to introduce us to Melville and Fitzgerald, it was clear that Faulkner was her favorite. She loved telling us about *Yoknapatawpha* County, which Faulkner used as the setting for most of his books. Even saying the name, "*Yoknapatawpha*," gave her visible pleasure. She couldn't have been more enthusiastic when she read the soliloquy from Macbeth, and when we struggled to understand Benjy's section, she urged us to stop worrying about plot.

We complained, "How were we supposed to know that when he sees a caddie, he thinks about his sister Caddy?"

"Don't worry," she counseled, ever the cheerleader. "Just picture what he's picturing and read it out loud. Sometimes it helps to hear the words, not just see them on the page."

The only time she expressed any disappointment in us was when she learned we liked Jason, whose motivations (and narration) we understood better than Quentin, whose motivations (and narration) didn't make any sense at all.

"Quentin is intelligent and passionate and sensitive," Mrs. Zimbalist said. "And Caddy was Quentin's best friend. He is devastated by her disgrace. Imagine how you'd feel if you lost the person you loved most."

She encouraged us to reread those two sections so we'd have a better understanding of the characters and the themes of the book. Of course, none of us reread anything. We believed she had given us the answers, and that's all we needed to complete the final paper on *The Sound and the Fury*. We had lots of homework in other classes, plus SATs to prepare for and didn't have time to do extra work. If it wasn't going to help our GPA, then it didn't matter.

By the time we were seniors, we thought we knew Mrs. Zimbalist pretty well. We were used to her habit of color-coordinating running shoes and calf-length Talbot's shirt-dresses. We respected her place in the teacher pecking order. She didn't rank quite as high as Mrs. Worth, the strict taskmaster we all feared and revered, but definitely higher than Mr. Posterns, who assigned as few papers as possible and was a bartender on weekends.

Perhaps, most of all, we were proud of the way we had learned to make good use of Mrs. Zimbalist's tenuous class management capabilities, knowing it was fairly easy to throw her off track.

Christina Lesseur was especially good at luring Mrs. Zimbalist into talking all class so that we didn't have to do any work. Around the time we were supposed to be reading *A Separate Peace*, Christina was knee-deep in the yearbook crisis. She was co-editor of the yearbook with Susie Park. They were best friends, so working together on layout and design had been lots of fun, but once it became clear that Christina had a shot at Yale while Susie did not, things got ugly between them. Just before the final layout was due, Susie made a wreck of the whole thing and Christina had to spend days and days redoing it. With all this going on, she didn't have time to read a book about a war that happened before she was born. So the day Mrs. Zimbalist announced a pop quiz, Christina had to think fast.

"Mrs. Zimbalist," she began with wide-eyed innocence, "I'm not sure I understand the theme suggested by the title of the book."

Mrs. Zimbalist looked at her for a minute and then launched into a diatribe about the nature of friendship, the human tendency to be competitive, and the value of forgiveness. By the time her speech wound down, the class was almost over. Christina's quick thinking had worked. There was no time left for a quiz.

There is no question that it was Mrs. Zimbalist's easy-going, easy-to-manipulate ways that led us to pull a prank on her that beautiful spring afternoon. A prank she didn't deserve, but senior pranks were a school tradition, I kept telling myself ever after.

Legend had it that the VW Beetle prank in *A Prayer for Owen Meany* was inspired by something that once happened at our school. While our class didn't quite have the hutzpah (or the strength) to carry a car into the auditorium, we were pretty proud of what we accomplished. After the first football game in September, we snuck into the school building in the middle of the night to move the principal's office furniture into the second floor boys' bathroom.

On the Tuesday before Christmas, we had

hidden an alarm clock in each room of the school, set to go off at 10:46 a.m. It had taken a fair amount of work to collect the required number of clocks and find an appropriate place for each one, but the resulting chaos was well worth the effort.

The prank we pulled on Mrs. Zimbalist was different. It required no stealth and no planning. We didn't have endless arguments about who would do what. Instead, it came to us all rather spontaneously at the beginning of one of the last classes of the year.

Our English class took place right after lunch, which meant we would straggle in bit by bit, rather than arriving all at once, as we would have if we had rushed into the room directly from another subject. It was not unusual for many of us to arrive early.

Earlier in the year, students who arrived early would have spent their time hastily finishing homework or getting a head start on work due the next day. But with only a few days before graduation, no one really cared. College decisions had been made and grades were almost final. There was nothing to do but enjoy the beautiful day and pull one final class prank.

It wasn't until later that I realized that with this prank, I got more than I bargained for.

Mrs. Zimbalist's classroom overlooked the school's courtyard. It was a pretty, grassy space between the main building and the football stadium. On this particular day, the classroom windows were wide open to take advantage of the balmy breeze.

This was long before the days of child-proofing. There were no screens or window guards and it was a long way down from the fourth floor.

Without too much discussion, Peter Morris ran downstairs, into the courtyard, and lay on the ground beneath the window. The prank wasn't his idea. In fact, it isn't clear where it started, but Peter knew exactly what to do. He lay perfectly still once he had arranged his body in the sort of crumpled position that he felt approximated a fall from above. The rest of us stood at the windows and performed the role of hysterical onlookers, with an abundance of screaming. Maybe even a few tears.

When Mrs. Zimbalist entered the room and checked the view, her face blanched fully white. "It's happened again," she whispered. Mascara streaks striped her face. Tears dripped off her chin. She stood there for a moment, the outline of her body blocking the sunlight from the room. With heaving chest and tear-stained cheeks, she hitched her skirt and carefully placed sneaker-clad feet on the window sill. And then, without another word, she was gone.

In the days that followed, we learned a number of things. They assured us her death was almost instantaneous.

She landed on top of Peter and broke every rib in his body. One punctured his lung and he's never fully recovered.

We learned that Mrs. Zimbalist's teenage son committed suicide by jumping from that very window some years before.

The oozing blood that emptied out of her head onto the concrete will remain partly visible for a long time to come.

Our screams and tears were real that time, and the memory hasn't faded yet.

***

Backpack Buddies

by Kathleen M Fisher
Short Story Contest Finalist 2015

"Stop following me!" George yelled. He was running now, weaving wildly across the sidewalk, a wheeled-backpack jostling along behind him. Just three more houses and he would be at his front door.

His mom was right. "Be careful around stray animals," she had said. "You might get more than you bargain for."

George had been at the new school two weeks. All he really "bargained for" was to fit in. To make friends.

Instead the boys in his fifth grade class teased him for using a wheeled backpack, the kind with a pull handle that extends so you don't have to wear it on your back.

Seth, the tall kid with curly blond hair and arms the size of baseball bats, called it a "wheelchair."

How was George supposed to know that fifth graders in Creekside Falls no longer used wheeled backpacks? Everyone in his old hometown did. George missed it. A lot.

To top it off, the whole school was in an uproar because sports trophies kept disappearing from the school office. That mystery started right after Mr. Holt, the old basketball coach left, and right about the time George arrived. Guess who Seth and crew said was to blame?

And now, a three-legged 50-pound Godzilla was chasing George home. This was way more than he bargained for.

Maybe Godzilla was a stretch. It was really just a mangy black and white dog, about the size of the sea turtles George saw at the zoo. It reminded him of his grandpa's cow dogs but with shorter hair and floppier ears. He had seen the dog often hanging around the school.

Mrs. Wiley, his teacher, said it was a stray and that before Mr. Holt left, he would feed it and let it come in the gym to stay warm during basketball practices. Now Mr. Holt was gone but the dog was not.

Today when George left, he saw the mutt lying in the shade. It looked sad. He felt sorry for the dog. He knew how it felt to lose your best friend. He reached down to pet it. It seemed to like that. But then when George left, the dog followed.

That just fueled the jeers from Seth and his crew. Seth looked more like the seventh and eighth graders than a fifth grader. As George left the parking lot, he heard "Oh look, George has his old dog with him today. With only three legs. He must need a wheelchair too. George, don't forget to get soft food for you and your dog. Y'all need a snack you can chew."

George ignored the dog at first. But then it started to bark at him and to follow faster and bark louder. So George started running.

His backpack bumped awkwardly along behind him as he took the stairs of his front porch two at a time. Cymbal, his grey tabby cat was lounging lazily on the porch swing. *Good*, George thought. *Cymbal will scare the dog off.*

He slammed the front door and was leaning against it breathing heavily. He felt something brush his legs and jumped. But it was just Cymbal. Somehow she had snuck in as he hastily pulled his backpack through the open door. So much for scaring away the monster creeping up behind him. He could hear the dog hobbling up the steps. It scratched and barked at the door. *Maybe if I ignore it, it will go away*, George thought.

His mom called from the kitchen. "Georgie, is that you? Come in the kitchen. I made cookies. I want to hear about your day."

George hated that name! He imagined what Seth would say if he heard that!

The thought of mom's homemade chocolate chip cookies made George's mouth water. The noises from the dog faded in importance. He parked his backpack and ran to the kitchen.

"How was school today?" Mom asked. "Any word on what's going on with the missing trophies?"

"It was fine," George said between mouthfuls of cookie. "The trophies are still a mystery. Ever since Mr. Holt left and they announced the new basketball team, one trophy has disappeared each day. Nobody can figure it out."

He paused then added, "That kid, Seth, in my class keeps joking and saying I'm hauling them off in my backpack because they started missing when I came. I know he is joking but I wish he wouldn't say it. Just think," he continued, "if I could solve that mystery, then who would be the joke?"

"Aww George, I'm sorry," Mom said. "I know it's hard to make friends at a new school, especially when everything is so different. But give it time. Sometimes friends turn up in the unlikeliest of places. And who knows, maybe you are just the detective they need on the case!"

There she goes again, George thought. *Mom has a saying for everything*. But after a few of her cookies and a cold glass of milk, George felt better. Maybe he would solve the case and be the hero of Creekside Falls Elementary. His first decree as the hero would be to make all kids use wheeled backpacks.

George headed upstairs to start his homework. He got so busy that he completely forgot about the missing trophies and Godzilla at the door.

The next morning when George opened the front door to leave, there was the dog. That crippled fleabag had slept all night right there on the front porch! George couldn't believe it. Fortunately he wasn't barking, but George thought he looked hungry.

He ran in the house to get some food. He glanced around the kitchen. Lucky Charms? A piece of bread? A banana? Then he saw Cymbal's plastic bin of cat food. Well, it wasn't exactly dog food, but Mom would probably flip if she saw him sneaking Lucky Charms out to a dog.

George eased slowly back out onto the porch. Still no barking. That must be a good sign. George set the bowl down and backed toward the house. Within seconds the dog began sniffing his way toward the bowl. Tentatively at first, then with more gusto, the three-legged beast scarfed down every morsel.

Wow, he must be hungry, George thought. *I wonder how long since he last ate?* It was a little easier to feel sorry for this beast now that it didn't seem to be screaming at him. He wondered what in the world made the dog so determined to get his attention yesterday and why he would hang around another day.

George was still thinking about this as he wheeled his backpack down the sidewalk toward school. As he rounded the corner toward the entrance, he realized he wasn't alone. The dog was following him. Again.

This time George had to know what was going on. He stopped and reached down to pet the dog. He scratched lightly between his crazy ears.

The dog started to lick his hand and then to bark as if he wanted attention.

Here we go again, George thought.

Just then the dog darted off around the school. He moved fast for only having three legs.

George was stunned. He stood there wondering what happened. After about 30 seconds, he shrugged and started toward the front doors.

But the dog came back, barking at him louder, and then he turned and ran off again.

George couldn't resist the curiosity. He turned to follow the dog. It was as though this dog was pulling him by an invisible leash.

They passed the main school doors, the side door to the cafeteria and then continued on toward the playground. They were headed behind the swings toward the shed where the school kept lawn mowers and big equipment.

George had never been over here before, and he was pretty sure it was off limits to students. He hesitated but just as he was about to turn back, he saw someone tiptoeing into the shed. It was a student. A student with curly blond hair and baseball bat arms. Seth! What was he doing going in the maintenance shed?

The dog continued barking and making sure George was following. As they got close to the shed, the door flung open, and George found himself face to face with Seth!

"What are you doing here?" both boys said simultaneously.

"Well, I'm here because this dog seemed to think I needed to come out here. I have no idea why," George said. "But what were you doing?" he added with a frown.

Seth looked like he was up to no good. He hung his head. "I," he paused. Then he sighed and started again, "I... oh just go in and look, will you?" He pointed toward the half-closed door to the shed.

George walked in and saw it immediately. A whole box full of none other than the missing sports trophies! There they were. It had to be all of them. They were spilling over the sides of the box.

"I don't understand," George said as he came back out. "How did those get in here? And how did you know they were here? And why haven't you told anyone this is where they were? And why did you keep saying I took them?"

"I'm sorry," Seth said still looking at the ground. He kicked the sidewalk with the toe of his sneaker. "When I got cut from the basketball team, I was just so mad I thought I could really get back at the coaches by hiding all their trophies. Are you gonna tell?" He looked up at George.

George didn't know what to do. He knew it would be wrong not to tell somebody, but he couldn't help but feel sorry for Seth. He knew how it felt to be excluded. He looked from Seth to the dog. "Was this what you were trying to tell me?" he asked the pooch. "Did you know it was Seth and you wanted me to find the trophies?"

His mom's words tumbled back into his brain. "Sometimes you find friends in the unlikeliest of places. And sometimes you get more than you bargain for."

"I have an idea," George exclaimed as a grin spread on his face. He turned to Seth and said, "Help me load these trophies into my backpack. We'll wheel them back to school together. We'll tell everyone we followed this dog around the back of the school and happened to find the trophies."

"You mean you aren't gonna rat me out?" Seth asked. "After all the mean things I said about you and your backpack and your dog?"

My dog, George thought. *I like the sound of that.* Maybe being a little different wasn't all that bad. Maybe having a wheeled backpack wasn't all that uncool. And maybe a three-legged friend could be just as good as a two-legged friend.

"No," George said. "But YOU are going to be the one to pull the backpack. I have to get some water for my new dog."

"Me? Pull that backpack? Oh, all right," Seth grumbled. He paused. Then he added, "Thanks, George. Thanks for being a good friend. I'm sorry for the things I said."

Once again, Mom was so right, George thought. *I now have not one, but two good friends. I got more than I bargained for!*

***

A Rough Goodbye

by Victor Espinosa
Short Story Contest Finalist 2015

Logan pulled the Jeep into the drop off lot and checked his phone. One message flashed across the screen. *Are you sure about this?* It was his girlfriend, Leah, trying to discourage him. He looked toward the empty launch point and rushing waters just beyond, then nodded, more to convince himself than that he was ready to offer a response.

He typed in one word – *Yes* - stuffed the phone into his waterproof bag, and stepped into the chilly morning air. His breath floated in the breeze as he locked the Jeep and tossed his keys in the waterproof bag.

Nearby swirling rapids called to him as they pounded on the rocks below with deafening agony. He swallowed hard, untied the raft on the Jeep's roof and claimed his gear. Without taking his eyes off the river, he climbed into gear and cinched the life jacket tight.

"I can do this. I can do this. I *must* do this," he muttered in soft affirmation.

Shoulder muscles groaned as he dragged the orange raft across gravel and onto the cement launch point.

Oh, man. I can't believe I almost forgot him.

Logan fumbled for the keys and jogged back to the Jeep. A small airtight container lay on the passenger seat. Theo. Just two weeks earlier, its contents had been his best friend. "Sorry, buddy," he said, and strolled back to the launch point. He tied Theo and his container down, stowed the keys, secured the waterproof bag, and pulled the raft into the water.

He had never experienced anything remotely close to what he was about to attempt. Theo had always been the lively, active one, even going so far as to open his own rafting company while Logan played it safe and used fragile health as an excuse. Now that his friend was gone, he would have to learn how to function independently.

I'll live more like you, buddy. I'll make you proud of me. I'll spread your ashes on the Colorado River as you requested, but you gotta stay with me, at least in spirit, 'cause I'm in over my head. He shook his head at what might turn out to be a good pun, but if so, he wouldn't be there to enjoy the laugh. He may really be in over his head before the day was out.

The frigid water sent a chill up his spine. What a pansy. He inhaled sharply. "Stay with me, partner," he said aloud and then looked up. "I haven't even started and I'm wimping out. No, you don't, Logan. You're gonna do this for Theo."

He seated himself inside, already frozen to the core. After one longing look at the warm Jeep, he pushed off the bank. The water took his raft immediately and sucked it down to a collection of boulders.

He flew through the first set of rapids without putting his paddle in the water, and was whipped towards the second set with incredible speed. Boulders loomed toward him, and he struck at the water with his paddle. The raft turned lazily, like an old mare that had been put out to pasture, and then slipped seamlessly between two monolithic stones covered in moss.

"This is insane!" Logan shouted to himself, Theo, and the river as he pelted downstream. Various sized obstacles dominated his view as he calculated the best way to stay alive. Before the day was over, he may end up in the afterlife with Theo.

His heart thumped against his chest, as though trying to escape. He practiced negotiating upcoming debris and jutting rocks. Sometimes he didn't make his mark. Sometimes he slammed into rocks, shifted and spun, and careened downhill faster than his mind could match, and all the time, adrenaline flooded his system and his heart banged in his eardrums.

Trees and healthy brush along the riverbank rushed past in a blur. The raft crashed into an underwater rock and he vowed to control his movements with more precision lest he tear the bottom out.

He began to get the hang of it. "Ha! Look at that, buddy," he said as he paddled. "This isn't so hard. A level five river, huh. This is easy!" A bend in the river revealed a small waterfall that preceded jagged stones and murky depths. "Uh oh, I take that back."

The orange raft sailed into the air and slammed back into the drink with surprising force. Water rushed over the top and soaked him to the bone, making his legs frigid and stiff, his hands numb… just before an underwater branch snared him. Hung in the branches, his momentum ceased but the flow of water didn't, and the river swallowed his raft eagerly. He was up to his chest in the torrent.

A frightened yelp escaped. Logan stabbed at the branch with his paddle, well aware it was do or die. The branch bowed but held fast. He gasped for air, held his breath and hacked away at the limbs. They buckled underwater and released him to the greater strength of the river.

Catapulting away from one danger and toward another, he yelled, "Theo!" Slashing freezing water splashed into his face, temporarily blinding him. "I think I may have …" His raft slammed into a rock and the force disconnected his words. "I think I definitely …" Rapids bucked against his raft and sent him careening toward a second waterfall. His eyes opened wide in terror. "Theo, buddy, I got more than I bargained for. Save me a seat up yonder." He shut his eyes and held onto the paddle with all his might.

Icy water crashed into him and knocked the breath out of his lungs with cold efficiency. He wiped his face and floated into a calm, pristine area where he could clearly see the bottom. The still surface expertly disguised the current beneath. As

Logan began to paddle across the peaceful reprieve, he startled a camouflaged duck, which took to the air, quacking. He smiled.

"Perfect. This is the perfect spot," he said. He unscrewed the lid to Theo's container and gently sprinkled the gray contents along the side of his raft. What he hoped would be a simple, serene act turned into an emotional powerhouse as the ashes dissolved.

"I can't believe you asked for this," he said. Within seconds, the container was empty. His face felt like an artic breeze had frozen a gallon of water to his two-day beard, and yet he could somehow differentiate unending streams of warm, salty tears. He laid his head on the side of the raft and collapsed in sobs. At length, he looked back at the gray trail he left in the water. "I'm going to miss you, buddy."

A distant cry caught his ears and he turned forward. Down the river, past another collection of rapids, Logan could see the building that was Theo's rafting company. One car sat parked in its lot, and a person next to it stood waving. Leah. She waved, and no other wave had ever looked so good.

Logan wiped the tears from his eyes and headed toward the last set of obstacles. He didn't look back. Theo would have wanted it that way. From now on, he would look forward.

***

Miss Goins is Gone

by T.L. Needham
Short Story Contest Finalist 2015

My ears were numb from the machine-gun like explosions from the strings of firecrackers. We had set them off in the dark for over an hour at the corner crossroads where our gang gathered for the event. The racket and flash of the exploding fireworks was always a thrill. The fact that the fireworks were illegal added to the delight.

None of us could afford, nor were we allowed to have fireworks. Except Wesley, whose folks always bought him a big box through mail order. Yet Wesley, being the youngest and smallest in our gang, always allowed Charlie, my older brother, and his pal, Vern, to set off the fireworks for us younger boys. They would have done so anyway because no one could stop them.

"Wesley, you come home now," a voice shouted from up the street.

"I have to go home, Mom's calling me," Wesley said. "Must be bedtime."

He and I really enjoyed watching fireworks go off, but we both wished we could set them off ourselves.

Wesley stood up to walk up the block to his house. He paused and said with a sudden rush of fear, "What is that . . .?"

I stood up quickly and turned around. We were standing on the darkest corner of the intersection, the side without a street light overhead. He was gazing at the house on the corner, pointing his finger, with his jaw drooped open.

It was an old house, just like all the big homes in this neighborhood. But the weird thing about this house was that there were no lights on at all. Only total darkness inside the house.

"Look there . . ." Wesley whispered. The tone in his voice made me shudder.

Then I saw what he was seeing, what he was pointing at, what made him so frightened.
Each window on the front of the house was totally black. There was not a single light on in the entire house, except one tiny eerie red glow right in the middle of the picture window on the first floor. You could barely see it. Then, as I strained my eyes to focus on and understand what this tiny red glow was, it expanded for an instant and suddenly grew brighter, and then subsided back to its normal glow. It seemed to breathe. It was alive!

I looked at Wesley in amazement. Something in the dark old house was watching us out that window.

"I'm going home," Wesley cried, as he took off running down the block.

I looked back at the light. It still just glowed but did not breathe brighter again.

"What's going on?" Charlie asked, as he and Vern walked up behind me.

I realized now that all the other kids had gone home. It was getting late, and bedtime had already passed. I said nothing, not wanting to show my fear like Wesley, so Vern and Charlie would not torment me, or make fun of me for being a coward. I just turned around and pointed at the dark old house with the blacked-out windows, and the strange eerie glow of a small red light in the middle of the picture window.

In that instant, as all three of us peered at this tiny red glowing light, it breathed bright again. This made it seem so alive and that was very unnerving.

"That must be old lady Goins just sitting there in the darkness smoking a cigar. That's all," said Vern, sounding confident in his explanation.

"Are you sure?" Charlie asked. "Why are there no lights on in that house? And how come we've never seen anyone come or go from that old house? I've never even heard of old lady Goins."

"I've never seen her either. No one has as far as I know. She's very old and she's lived in that house longer than anyone who lives around here can remember. But she 's blind and smokes cigars. That's what my dad says, and he knows all about her because he works at the grocery store. She has her food delivered to the house once each week," Vern explained, proud of himself for having information no one else had.

There was another flare-up of the red glowing light. "Let's go knock on her door and see what happens!" Charlie said, with mischievous glee in his voice.

"Won't do any good. She's deaf, too," Vern added.

"Bull! You're making all this up," Charlie said, giving Vern a punch on the shoulder.

"Charlie! You boys come home . . . NOW!"

"That's Mom calling us, Charlie, we better get home," I said. I took off running home to put distance between me and that creepy old *Goins* house. Within a few minutes I was snug in my bed, under the covers.

The next morning as I set off on my walk to school, I looked around, but no other kids were in sight. Maybe I was early, or late—whatever, but I kept going. I got down to the corner, the one we would now call *Goins' Corner*, and thought about the creepy old lady who smoked cigars. Her house did not look so creepy in broad daylight. Then I noticed that the front door was standing wide open. A black funeral hearse was parked at the curb.

I stopped and stared into the open door. I saw two men pick up something, no, someone, covered with a large white sheet and place them on a gurney. Then they rolled the gurney with the sheet-covered body out the front door, onto the porch, and down the sidewalk toward the waiting hearse.

"Who's that?" I asked, feeling more than a little creepy again.

"Sonny, this is Miss Goins. She passed away last night. Poor old thing was over 100-years old. Deaf and blind all her life. Grocery delivery boy found her first thing this morning, sitting in her rocking chair right there in front of that big picture window," one of the men explained as they loaded the shrouded remains of old Miss Goins into the hearse. "Yep, old Miss Goins is gone," he said, as he slammed the back door of the hearse.

As I walked to summer school, my dream about Miss Goins buzzed in my mind. I spent the entire day thinking about poor old Miss Goins. Sitting there in the darkness, which for her was never ending, in silence—an eternal silence now, I guess. I wondered so many things. How did she manage? What would it be like to not see or hear anything? Must be a lot like being dead all the time. And did she really die? She couldn't see or hear what we were doing last night in front of her house… our noisy fireworks war zone. Unless somehow she felt it, all the loud bursts, exploding fast. Maybe we upset her. I couldn't get her out of my mind.

After it was dark and everyone had gone to bed, and the neighborhood was quiet, I found the courage to get up, get dressed and sneak out of the house. Some strange curiosity compelled me to go out of my own safe home, and walk down the street to old Miss Goins' house.

I don't really know why. It was like I was summoned, compelled, or beckoned to come in the darkness again to the creepy old house of this strangely afflicted and mysterious old lady. Finally I reached her front gate. I stood there looking at the dark old house with all the windows blacked-out, no light coming from within at all. My eyes were drawn to the big picture window. Nothing. Not like last night. No eerie, red, breathing glow. I don't know what I expected, but I felt a gentle release of my fear, a reassurance that all was right, and good, and okay, just as it should be.

And then it happened! The red glow… it was still there! It seemed as if old Miss Goins was sitting in her chair near the window and took a big draw on her cigar. It breathed, glowing bright red again, just as the night before, then back down to the steady glow.

I felt goose bumps rise on my arms and felt the hair on the back of my neck stand straight up. My heart pounded and my body shivered with a frightful chill. How can it be? What was making that strange, eerie, red glowing light? Miss Goins is gone… she's dead. I saw them take her away… didn't I? Coming back here, I got more than I bargained for.

I ran home as fast as my feet would move. I quietly slipped back into my house, up the stairs and climbed into my own bed. I slept the rest of the night with my blanket over my head, my bedroom door closed and window latched. I slept that way until I left home for college. Just in case.

***

Paid in Full

by Victor Atterbury
Short Story Contest Finalist 2015

It was another ice cold morning in Kimberly, South Africa, where thin layers of ice covered the swimming pool that glistened in the morning sunlight. Spencer Venter sat in his room looking at the pool, but not really seeing it. His mind peeled back to the incident of the previous week until a knock at the door brought him back to reality.

"Spence, we've got to go, son."

The young teen didn't answer. He pulled on polished shoes and walked down the corridor to the living room. The corridor seemed longer today, and a low murmur rode up the steps to greet him. The living room was packed with people. He knew most, but others were total strangers. Spence's father stood at the end and waited for a settling calm.

"I want to thank everyone for coming today. It is with great sadness that we are joined, but she would have appreciated your attendance, and so do Spencer and I." The recitation went on.

Wasn't it enough that she was dead, without having to speak to every person present?

A convoy of vehicles parked along the driveway and halfway down the street. Black seemed to be the color of the day, except for the woman wearing the garish red dress. Maybe she belonged at the party down the block. It seemed every third person hid behind a pair of sunglasses. How weird was that?

At some point, the recitation ended. Someone took Spence by the arm and led him to a black limousine. Mom never liked black, and this was no time to be hobnobbing with strangers. What kind of person expected him to hold polite conversations when he was choking on his own spit?

Go away, people. Go away.

"Good morning, Mr. Venter. Would you mind if I ride with you and Spencer? I thought maybe I could… you know… be there for him if he feels like talking."

"Good morning, Samantha. Of course. I appreciate the offer. How about you two wait here while I tie up a couple of loose ends?"

Spencer looked at her with vacant eyes, not registering her faint smile, blue eyes or light brown hair. Not noticing the Passion perfume she was wearing. Not even feeling the pain in her heart on his behalf. He did feel the warmth of her hand pulling him into the limo.

"Spencer, are you okay?"

He should nod, shouldn't he? Or maybe even say something, but there was nothing to say that day. A tear gathered and was about to spill over Samantha's eye. How strange that she should cry. It wasn't her mother. Tears wouldn't come for him. Maybe they never would. Samantha's hand still held his. Did they usually hold hands? He couldn't remember.

"Spencer. Are you okay, son?" his father said.

What a stupid question. *Was he okay? Was he okay? No. Hardly. He would never be okay again.*

Dad's eyes brimmed with tears that balanced on the edge of his eyelids. "I need you son. Hang on. We'll get through this."

Samantha placed her arm around his shoulder and leaned in close to whisper. "It's going to be okay. I'm here."

Spencer looked at her. No. It wasn't okay. Nor would it ever be okay again. Not ever. A whirling black abyss was swallowing him. Couldn't anyone else see it? He was drowning. Drowning. Drowning.

The limo bumped along a curvy road and maniacs stopped to stare. At some point, Samantha tugged on his arm again.

"Come on, Spence. I'm with you."

He yielded to the tug.

They seemed to be in the graveyard now. Lots of dead people. Lots. Family, friends, and strangers poked across one grave after the other like a slow troupe of baby elephants.

Spencer wondered if he was walking on the heads or feet of those underground. They shouldn't mind.

Samantha guided him to a chair. Why were most people standing? She sat next to him in the blue and white gazebo and the fragrance of her perfume flowed over him like a summer breeze.

This must be hell, he thought. Spencer gazed at the red soil peeping beneath a fresh snow. Kind of pretty, actually. He never noticed that before. How strange that he should notice it now.

Samantha gripped his fingers, and somehow, he squeezed her hand. People filed by the gravesite while he sat and shivered. She pulled him toward the grave.

No. I don't want to go.

She pulled again.

If I must.

It was a pretty coffin. Mom would like it. Beneath the casket lay a gaping hole, waiting to gulp her body.

They would cover the grave. The snow would melt and spring would eventually come. Sod would cover the grave, and someday another godforsaken soul would tread across her grave to drop their loved one into the hungry ground.

"Dear family and friends. We are gathered together for one last farewell to a wonderful wife and mother. Elizabeth wanted to leave a quick message of love to her family. She wanted them to celebrate her life rather than mourn her death. She left this note."

To my husband and son. I write this note with a heavy heart. I must accept this, and you must, too. This is the way it was meant to be. You filled my life with abundant love and exuberant happiness, and we will be together again one day. Take care of each other. Live each day as though it's your last. I will love you throughout eternity.

Samantha pulled on his hand.

No. He couldn't. He stood looking down on the casket. One knee collapsed, and then the other. One tear fell. Then two. Then a river of tears. A river that would never end. Then an uncontrollable cry that sounded like a scream from Hades shook both loved ones and friends. Was it his cry? Compassion spread through the crowd as one began to sob and then another and another.

Now on his hands and knees, the boy crawled to the edge of the grave. His tears dripped onto the coffin. "Mommm. Mommm," he wailed. "Forgive me. Forgive meee."

Samantha knelt next to him. "It wasn't your fault," she said.

"Yes, it was."

"Mr. Venter?" Samantha raised a questioning face to the gent. "Why does he blame himself?"

Forest Venter knelt by her side and spoke low. "He asked if he could meet you at the park last week. His mother said no, that she might not be strong enough. He had a fit and said he hoped she would really get sick. He had no idea how sick she really was. She died the next day."

"Oh, Spence. Your mom was dying of cancer. She would have died anyway."

"I wish I'd never said it. I didn't mean it. I was just mad, but when I wished that illness on her, I got more than I bargained for. And now she's gone and I can't bring her back. I can't …"

"Spencer. Listen to me." Samantha placed both her hands on his face and turned it to her. "Now look me in the eye. You are not responsible.

What you said happened after she was already ill. She knew she was sick, but she and your father kept it from you. You would have never said such a think if you'd known. You could have had an amazing last couple of weeks with her if they had told you, but they thought they were sparing you pain. You have to forgive them, but more than that, you have to forgive yourself."

Exactly one year later, Spencer walked to his mother's gravesite. With a clean handkerchief, he wiped the dust off the tombstone.

A dark figure slipped noiselessly across the sod and jammed a knife against the boy's ribs. "Give me your money and that watch, boy!"

He felt no fear. "Here's the money, but I'll die before you get this watch. It was the last gift I received from my mother."

"I said gimme the watch!"

"No!" Spencer grabbed at the knife-wielding arm. A sharp, stinging pain to the abdomen dropped him to his knees. He clutched his ribs and stared at scarlet fingers. Spencer's head tilted toward the bright sky and a smile crossed his face as his eyes closed.

"I see you, Mom."

***

Terror on the Gulf

by Rosanne Gulisano
Short Story Contest Finalist 2015

Melissa Cooney snuggled deep in her deck chair as the converted lobster boat pitched in gentle waves. She sighed with contentment, feasting on the soft night. "Can you think of another place on earth you'd rather be?" she said.

Her mother, Maddie, smiled. "Fairhope is a little slice of heaven. I don't know when I've seen so many stars. It looks like a fisherman cast his net and released them into the heavens."

Cliff DeGeorge was at the helm, reveling his role as a sailor. This was the man Melissa now called Pop, her mother's second husband, and tonight the three would adventure together on *The Tadpole*.

"You ladies comfortable back there?"

"We're fine, dear. All set for the night," Maddie said.

Cliff dropped anchor and joined them. "I think we had a pretty good day for a first cruise in the old tub."

"It's been a wonderful day, dear. I loved cooking in the cute little galley. This boat will be like a second home. I can't wait to sail away with you… anywhere you want to go."

"Watch it, honeymooners," Melissa said. "There's a third wheel here, you know."

"Well, what do you expect from newlyweds?" her mother said.

"Pop, did you really buy this boat for a dollar?" Melissa said.

"Yup. Got her from an old army buddy. We christened her last week. She's large and decidedly ugly, but we have enough room to stand up below deck, good sleeping quarters, a galley and a bathroom with a shower. Your mom wanted something a bit more glamorous, but I couldn't pass up a deal like this."

"We polished, painted and refurbished and bought new equipment for the galley." Maddie studied the horizon. "Cliff, are you sure it isn't going to storm? The water is white-capping and I thought I saw lightening in the distance."

"Not to worry. You're in safe hands. The storm will pass us to the north and travel west."

"Don't be over-confident, Mr. Sailor. There! See that? Lightning. And see how the stars are fading," Maddie said.

Cliff straightened his broad shoulders and wiped wet brown hair from his face. "Just leave it to the menfolk and do your chores in the galley," he said, pushing bleached blonde hair out of her face.

"I beg your pardon," she said with indignity.

Cliff chuckled. "Just pushin' your buttons, darlin'. You don't have to stay in the galley. You can mend my socks and do my laundry instead." His face wreathed in smiles.

"I see we have a few things to work out, Mr. Wonderful." She paused. "Did you hear that? It sounded like a horn."

Cliff's brow furrowed in that gut-wrenching moment. They were too close to the shipping lane! "This would be a good time to pray," he said as the waves soared ever higher. "There's a barge out there, and he's warning us to get out of the way. Take the helm while I pull up anchor!"

"I can't drive a boat!"

"Just turn the wheel like you would on a car," he said, moving with surprising agility for a sixty-five year old. "This is no time to argue, my dear. Let's do that later."

The lights on the faraway barge loomed ever closer as the captain repeatedly blasted the horn. Water slopped onto the boat's deck and made it slick. Pots and pans clattered in the galley and Melissa's stomach tilted with the waves.

"Melissa!" Cliff's voice rose sharp against the wind. Now he shouted. "Get the life jackets."

A crack of thunder and a huge flash of lightning lit up the water. As the night turned inky black and rain started to pelt, Cliff wrangled with the anchor. The gale blew across the bow. Rain slashed their faces, and the boat bobbed like a cork. "Maddie! Tie that rope around your waist. Melissa, get another rope." He bellowed now.

"What about you? If you fall overboard, what would we do?" Melissa said.

"Can you tie a decent sailor's knot?"

"It's been a long time," she shouted back, "but I think I remember."

"Well, do it then, and do it quickly."

The barge's horn streaked through the air with a hideous roar.

"The anchor's lodged!"

"Pop, cut the rope. Cut the rope. She's gonna hit us."

A bullhorn sounded again. "Clear the lane. Clear the lane. This is your last warning."

Cliff grabbed the knife on his belt and sawed at the rope.

Maddie screamed. "Watch out! Here it comes! Hurry!"

"I'm hurrying. I'm hurrying." The knife was overmatched by the rope. "I love you," he screamed over the storm.

Maddie paled and began to cry.

The knife sawed through strands of strength all too slowly and all at once, split into two parts. Cliff ran to the helm and cut hard to portside. The Tadpole responded with sluggish energy, spun like a top, straightened and puttered away from death's door. The huge barge blasted its horn once more as crew members swore at them.

It was a night to remember. The raging storm blew through as quickly as it had enveloped them. The three stood on deck with arms around each other, watching it pass into the shadows of night. The adrenaline rush had come and gone, and they were drained of all energy.

Cliff's voice seemed too loud now. "Well, what can I say, my darlings? This is quite a maiden voyage. I got more than I bargained for tonight, that's for sure."

The exhausted trio clung to one another for a few moments of stunned silence as the barge returned to the shadows and the storm lit up the sky to the east. After offering a prayer of gratitude, Cliff rummaged for a spare anchor, and, away from the commercial shipping lane, lowered it. The three collapsed into chilling thoughts and their moments of terror on the Gulf of Mexico.

***

Focus

by Andrew Herd
Short Story Contest Finalist 2015

James watched as the tiny box in his hands began a slow flight from outstretched fingers over a street market stall. He tucked into a roll as he hit the ground, twisting his head to see where the box would clatter along the street. Cabbages from a stall went flying and landed around him with a leafy crunch.

"No!" James grunted as the precious box rolled toward the foot of a merchant. With lightning reflexes, he snapped it up and sprinted away beneath the watchful eyes of the stall owner. With every glance towards the tiny treasure, he deliberately knocked against other people and merchandise to cause chaos and confusion.

A muffled shout ahead pulled at his attention. He slid across the trestle of another fruit stand. Tomatoes and corn smeared across his pants and boots.

The cart owner stared at him slack-jawed as his eyes ranged from rage to a long, mournful stare at the mess left behind.

"Backgrounders," James panted. "They'll be the death of me." Between breaths, he addressed the box directly, "I thought you were supposed to be helping me."

As if to answer, a shout echoed above the noise of the market, each word as clear as though spoken from a foot away. "I see the thief!"

James' head turned to face the accuser and frowned.

At the top of the market street, the inspector locked eyes with him and stared with a clarity that none in the market could muster. The inspector turned to yell directions to his officers who seemed to appear out of thin air. A moment later the group ran down the hill while both merchants and townsfolk scattered to get out of the way.

With a heavy sigh, James looked at the box. "Really? I just stole you back and you're going to pull this on me? I hope you know that I won't make this easy." James careened back and forth down the wide street to knock over every cart he could. Angry shouts followed in his wake. In a few moments, he would be out of sight. The crisp, cold air burned against his teeth, soaked into his jaw, and down his throat. Each breath was more painful than the last.

James pulled around the corner into a side street and leaned into the side of a brick house. The line of sight between James and the inspector was broken. He waited a moment before he allowed himself to relax. "That was easier than I expected," James smiled at the box. "Out of sight, out of mind."

Moving the box to eye level, he held it gingerly by the sides so he wouldn't get cut again. The cube measured about an inch and half square, although the surface had been polished smooth by the touch of the hundreds who held it before him. The edges remained splinter sharp, defying logic and wisdom. The wood had been quarter sliced, making the age rings appear as solid, darkened bands. Between each band, tiny silver runes had been inlaid. As a whole, they looked like thin, broken lines of silver, too small to attempt to read without aid.

James caught a blur of motion out of the corner of his eye. He turned toward the main street entrance as a large body slammed into his side, knocking him to the ground.

The box went airborne and clattered down the alley.

"You should have run further, thief," the inspector's voice rang out, as clear as crystal.

"How? You were out of sight!" James pushed against the heavy officer on top of him and crawled toward the box. The weight of two officers piled onto him before he collapsed to the street.

The box rested just outside of his reach.

"Did you really think you could steal from the Viscount?" The inspector said as the officers hauled James to his feet and slapped handcuffs on him.

"I was only taking back what was mine," James said.

The inspector gazed at the little box on the ground. "This trinket belongs to the Viscount, not some petty thief." His eyes blinked as James' outline grew crisp against the officer's dull blur. "Very peculiar." He reached to pick up the box.

"So, that is what you wanted," James said. He broke into a large grin.

The inspector paused, his fingers just an inch from the box's smooth surface, and looked back at James. "What are you babbling about?"

"If you pick up the box, sir, you agree to the bargain. You will not like its terms."

"Get this loony out of here," the inspector yelled to the two officers holding James.

"This is your last warning. You can let me pick up the box, or you will suffer consequences you won't understand."

"I'm pretty sure I can handle a little box," the inspector smirked at James. "Hurry up," he snapped at his officers, "I don't want to see this thief again."

James laughed. His voice echoed off the walls to combine with other echoes, first growing softer, then louder, before fading away down the alley. "Don't worry. You won't see me again."

"The Viscount doesn't take lightly to thieves. I doubt you'll see anyone for a very, very long time."

James laughed again. "You've been warned."

Inspector Franklin snatched up the box and jerked back from the electric jolt that surged through his fingers, up his arm and washed over his body like a wave settling. As he shook his hand, a tingle of numbness spread from his fingertips. The box fell onto the alley stone with a hollow echo.

"What was that?" he yelled.

James replied, "The bargain, and its price. I hope you can handle it."

As Inspector Franklin watched, James' lively

green eyes faded to a dull, forgettable mud. Franklin blinked.

"What just happened to you?"

James just laughed.

The officers gripped him with unnecessary roughness. Inspector Franklin tried to call after them, but his head felt wooly with confusion and he couldn't think of their names. Not that they were important. He reached with hesitation towards the box again, expecting another jolt. Nothing happened this time.

"Just some static electricity, that's all. A stupid little trinket and a crazy thief spouting nonsense about a bargain have made my day." He stared at the box and its tiny silver runes. They appeared to glow under the sunlight. Unexpected warmth swept through his arm.

"You are a strange little thing," Franklin said, addressing the box.

The alley closed in on him, oppressive and watchful.

"Who's there?" Franklin whirled around and reached for his pistol with one hand, while holding the box in the other. Someone was watching him, making the hairs on his neck crawl. With slow, deliberate steps, he backed out of the alley into the market street, never taking his eyes from the alley.

"Sir, are we clear to leave?"

He spun on the two men, gun still drawn. "Where did you come from?"

"We've been here the whole time, sir," the second man said.

"What do you think you're doin', slippin' up on a man like that? Are you tryin' to get yourself shot?"

They stared at each other for a moment.

"Uh, sorry, sir."

The inspector cleared his throat, but couldn't clear his head. "I've retrieved the stolen goods. Catch up with …" He paused to think of the men's names and then pointed the gun in their direction, "the other two with the thief. Make sure he gets to the station."

The two saluted and melted into the crowd. What were the names of those two men? Why couldn't he think of them? He holstered his gun and turned his interest toward the box and the words that played back in his mind.

"What kind of bargain?" he murmured to the box. He blinked and laughed to himself. "I'm talking to a box. It's just a box. I'm goin' daffy."

The sky appeared dimmer now. The surrounding crowd dulled into indistinguishable people that surged closer, jostled and bumped him round about, all staring at the box.

"Here, watch it now!" he shouted.

Their eyes appeared larger. Their mouths wider.

"Break away now. Go about your own business or I'll have you hauled in," he said.

But down the street a bit, wasn't someone staring at him from the alley?

Taking large, sure steps, Franklin walked

back up the hill toward the Viscount's mansion carrying the little box. A single person stood out against the crowd of indifference. The man walked past the inspector, and cut a clear path through the crowd. The curious little man eyed the box, his features becoming richer and almost recognizable as he approached, and then faded again as he vanished from view.

An officer ran up to the inspector. "Sir, we've been looking for you," he said in a pant. "The thief escaped."

"What? How?"

"We don't know. One moment he was there, laughing his head off about how the box would find him again, and then he was gone."

Franklin recalled the man who had just walked past. "I might know where he went. Follow me."

The inspector sprinted down the street and after the man whose image had burned itself into his mind. The officer followed but soon fell out of sight, swallowed by the unfocused crowd. A single laugh echoed down the street, above the din of people, horses, and carts. Franklin located the source and followed the sound. The feeling of being watched pressed in, and forced him to cast glances over his shoulder as though being pursued.

Every eye in the growing crowd stared at him. Their features flickered brightly before returning to stages of monotony. The inspector moved into the shadows and moved from cover to cover through the street, lest he draw more attention. Sweat beaded on his brow as he stumbled over dustbin lids and onto the tail of a cat.

"What are you looking at?" he shouted at the crowd. They followed at a distance. Franklin swung his arm around and their heads swiveled to follow the worn little box. They pressed in. Waiting for something. Staring. Expecting... what? Inspector Franklin could still hear the vendors rattling off their spiels, as though everything was normal.

Franklin gripped the box until his fingers ached and panic sounded in his voice. "What are you?"

A voice rang out clear as crystal over the crowd. "The bargain can drive some people crazy. All that watching, day in and day out. It never ends. It can really wear on a person."

"That's the bargain?"

"In part," the voice said.

"Then I got more than I bargained for," he said.

An expectant hand reached out from the crowd, and Franklin dropped the box into it.

James caught the box as it dropped.

"What is it?" a man in the crowd asked as he stared at the box.

"You're in focus when you hold it. That's all I know. It's mine now," James said with a glint in his eyes, "forever and always." He pocketed the box and whistled as he walked away.

The crowd watched him, nudging each other, eyes narrowed.

***

~*~

If you enjoyed *Bargain! A Themed Anthology*,
please consider leaving a review on Amazon

If you would like to offer feedback, please email
jay@southernstarpublications.com

Thank you for reading this anthology.
~*~

Short story contest entries were judged on
originality, creativity, style and technique.
A great story can score well in the first two
categories but lose marks if grammar, punctuation
and spelling are incorrect and if paragraphs are
poorly formatted.
Learn how to write professionally by taking a
writing course. It could be the difference between a
top placement, being a finalist, or missing a top
spot.
With permission, the contest stories have been
edited for this publication while trying to maintain
the intent of the original entry.

Creative Writing Institute

Creative Writing Institute is an online writing school that provides a variety of writing courses where each student receives a private tutor. As a 501(c)3 nonprofit charity, we also sponsor cancer patients in free writing courses. In addition, we have attempted to construct our courses for visually impaired students who can use adaptive devices to enlarge or convert text into electronically synthesized speech.

Our goal: to rescue storm-tossed lives, and to escort students from their present level to their highest individual potential.

Our program has a three-tiered approach:

- We present professional material in a practical and simple method
- Private tutors personally escort students through the maze of unwritten rules and procedures
- At the end of the course, we evaluate students and recommend the next best choice on their ladder of learning

We will tailor your class to meet your needs. You will never be a number to us. We know all of our students on a first name basis. C'mon. Invest in yourself. Make it a priority. Dream big. We'll help you build a ladder to the stars!

Courses:

- Punctuation Review
- Creative Writing 101
- Dynamic Non-fiction
- Short Story Safari
- Writing for Children
- Writing for the Middle Grades
- Writing for the Young Adult
- Fantasy in Flight
- Horror House
- Fundamentals of Poetry
- Flash Fiction
- Novel Writing Made Easy
- Advanced Wordsmithing - coming soon
- Famous Women Poets - coming soon
- Writing Programs for the Blind

Payment plans available at no interest.

www.CreativeWritingInstitute.com/

Meet the Team

Creative Writing Institute is the place where people come together from all over the world. We pool knowledge and resources, and God makes miracles happen.

Some folks support this ministry financially, and our hearty thanks goes out to them. We also have volunteers who selflessly contribute time and talents. They come from all walks of life – ordinary homebodies, retired folks, and high school/college students. Most volunteers have full time jobs elsewhere, and yet they make time to help others. Our highest praise and thanks go to you.

The *Mystery Woman* planted the seed for CWI. If you read our "About Us" page, you will learn the story of how one woman riddled with cancer made a tremendous difference in the lives of others. Founder Deborah Owen read her story and decided if one woman could do all that, Creative Writing Institute could certainly carry her mantle and offer loving help to a hurting world.

We have workers in America, Canada, New Zealand, Africa, India, England, South Korea, Australia, and Italy. God bless those who have helped in the past, those who are helping now, and those who will stand by our side in the future.

Staff Members: in 2015, we rested from the arduous two-year building campaign and maintained. In 2016, we will build again. Courses under consideration are Memoir Writing, Technical Writing, and possibly more poetry courses. Thank you to staff members: Mrs. S. Joan Popek, Mr. E. Lynn Carroll, Mr. Joe Massingham, Mrs. Emily-Jane Hills Orford, Mrs. Kim Cawley, and Mrs. Diane Robinson. Welcome to our new Administrative Assistant, Ms. Michelle Malsbury, who also functions as the Newsletter Editor. Michelle is a dedicated volunteer whose amazing talent in designing makes our newsletter one of a kind.

Volunteer Staff: without these co-laborers to pick up the slack in the newsletter, library, blog posting, article writing and posting social media, we would not be able to keep up with the work. Thank you, William Battis (age 91!), Julie Canfield, Jianna Higgins, Nicky Hirst, Karen Johnson, Betty Crawford, Kevin Keeney, E. Lynn Carroll, Annette Griffin, and John Griffin. Others who helped in 2015 include Dr. Helen Tucker, Victoria Pakizer, Ariel Pakizer, Farheen Gani, Brent Middleton and Sola Johnson, to name a few. Whether or not your name is mentioned here, please accept our profuse thanks and appreciation!

Jay Hirst, publisher of Southern Star Publications: Thank you, Jay, for your many kindnesses and the hundreds of hours you volunteer annually. Thank you for being a punctual perfectionist, and for being easy to work with. Most of all, thank you for being *you*. Our anthology can be compared with anyone's and not come up lacking, all because of your painstaking efforts and leadership. We are delighted with your finished product.

Folks, when you need a publisher, check out **www.SouthernStarPublications.com**.

All for one, and one for all! God bless you, Team!

If you would like to be a part of this work, or if you would like to make a donation, please write to **DeborahOwen@CWinst.com**.